ABOUT THE AUTHOR

Maryam Master was born in Iran and moved to Australia when she was nine. She is a screenwriter and playwright who loves creating shows for young audiences.

Maryam has adapted three of David Walliams' books for the stage – *Mr Stink*, *Billionaire Boy* and *The Midnight Gang* – as well as Oliver Jeffers' *The Incredible Book Eating Boy*, all of which premiered at the Sydney Opera House and toured across Australia. She also collaborated with Australian Children's Laureate Leigh Hobbs on *Horrible Harriet: Live on Stage*.

She began her career in TV, writing for shows like *Home and Away*, *Blinky Bill* and the Jim Henson Company's *Bambaloo*. In 2011 she was selected by Sesame Workshop as the writer for Elmo's tour of Australia.

Exit Through the Gift Shop is her first novel.

EXIT THROUGH THE GIFT SHOP

MARYAM MASTER

Illustrated by ASTRED HICKS

Pan Macmillan Australia

Pan Macmillan acknowledges the Traditional Custodians of country throughout Australia and their connections to lands, waters and communities. We pay our respect to Elders past and present and extend that respect to all Aboriginal and Torres Strait Islander peoples today. We honour more than sixty thousand years of storytelling, art and culture.

First published 2021 in Pan by Pan Macmillan Australia Pty Ltd
1 Market Street, Sydney, New South Wales, Australia, 2000

Reprinted 2022 (four times), 2023

A catalogue record for this work is available from the National Library of Australia

Typeset in Basic Sans by Astred Hicks, Design Cherry
Cover, text design and illustrations by Astred Hicks, Design Cherry
Author photograph: Kate Williams Photography

Criminal Code Act 1995 on pages 129 and 130. Sourced from the Federal Register of Legislation at 27 May 2021. For the latest information on Australian Government law please go to https://www.legislation.gov.au.

Printed by IVE

The paper in this book is FSC® certified. FSC® promotes environmentally responsible, socially beneficial and economically viable management of the world's forests.

For Oli & Leo

So here's the thing . . .

I'm dying.

But **don't panic,**

it's not the end of the world!

Well, it's kind of the end of *my* world. But not yours. So

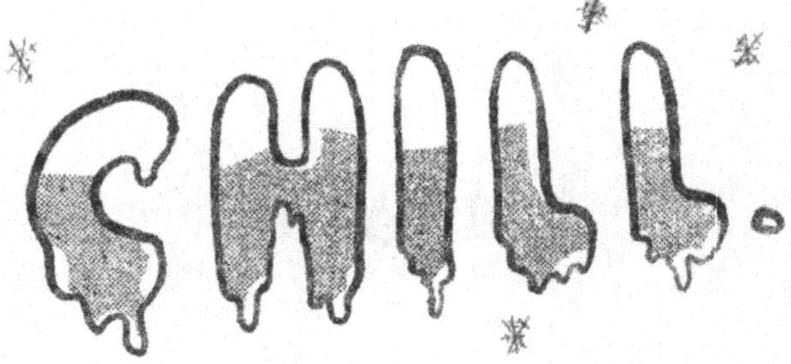

I know we're all going to die one day but according to Dr Needham, I've got about a year left. Give or take a bit. So, if that year were to begin today, in fact, right now, this very minute as I'm writing these words, I'll be dead by 11.43 am on 14 October next year. It's kind of spooky to have that sort of time limit put on your life. It's also sad.

And scary.

And surreal.

Surreal (suh-*reel*)
Adjective
When something is so weird and unbelievable that you feel like you're living in some kind of parallel universe or you're having one of those freaky dreams after you've eaten too many burritos for dinner.

Knowing approximately when and *how* you're going to die really messes with your head. Some days I swing from pure-panic-mode – 'This is not a drill! This is really happening!' – to calm-Zen-mode – 'Breathe in. Out. Accept the things you cannot change' – about a hundred times. Looping thoughts of life and death, death and life, buzz around my brain like there's some sort of malfunctioning microchip.

It's **exhausting.**

So yep, there it is. I'm dying.

But that's the least of my problems. My biggest problem at the moment can be described in two words.

Or 'Butt Breath' as I like to call her (not to her face, of course). Alyssa is the meanest of all mean girls.

Queen Mean.

If you kicked her in the heart, you'd probably break your toe. If my life was a Marvel movie, she would be the supervillain. But before I tell you about her (yes, she can wait, even though I'm sure she'd love to muscle in on EVERY part of my story), I should probably tell you about me. And all the good people in my life.

What's in a name? That which we call a rose . . .

Shakespeare wrote some gushy, romantic stuff about how names don't matter and a rose is a rose, and will still smell like a rose no matter what you call it. But I'm not buying that . . . I mean, would a rose really be as appealing if it were called 'pus-pie' or 'puke-petal' or just 'blurrrrgh'?

PUS-PIE

Yeah, I don't think so either. Which brings me to my name.

Anahita. No, not 'Anaconda', or 'And-a-heater' and definitely not 'Ana-hit-a-home-run'.

Anahita.

It's a pretty name.

It means 'Goddess of fertility and water' which is obviously cool. I'm down with any kind of goddess. But for some reason, no one seems to be able to say it. That 'hita' at the end just sends people into a spin. So I just go with Ana.

Disclosure: my full name is actually Anahita Rosalind Ghorban-Galaszczuk.

But don't try saying that

Really, don't.

This is me:

I'm a lot better looking in real life. This illustration is doing nothing for my complexion. I guess I am going through that awkward stage.

Puberty.

Or I think technically speaking, I'm pre-pubescent. Either way . . .

Blaaarrgh.

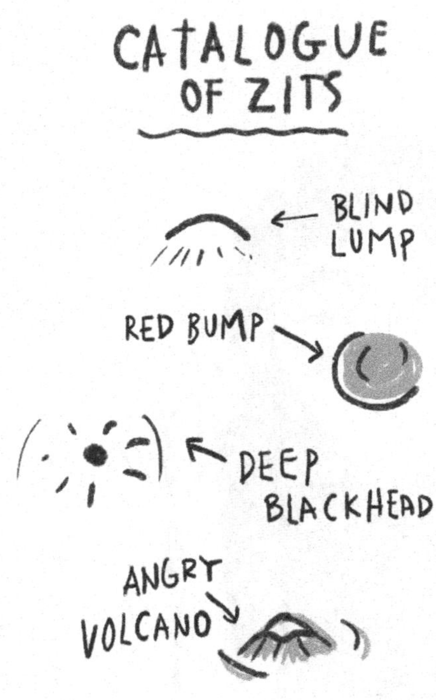

Is there anything worse? I mean, even the word 'puberty' sounds like something that you shouldn't say out loud. I'm not going to talk about all the hideous things that happen to teenage bodies during pu-u-u . . . (please refer to P word mentioned above) but I will say this: I have pimples (doesn't every 12.5-year-old?)

And my body hasn't quite grown into my nose yet.

Not that it matters. Or at least, that's what my mum has told me since I was zero.

'Looks are not important.'

'It's what's on the inside that counts.'

‘You are clever. You are creative. You are courageous. You are . . . you are . . . you are . . .’

It’s never-ending! My mum didn’t just read every ‘positive parenting’ book ever written, she wrote her own. I’m not just saying that. She actually did.

It’s called

The tagline was:

‘The secret to keeping your family together forever.’

Forever? Yeah, not so much. Just after the book was published my parents broke up. Painful, horrible, messy divorce.

But that’s another story.

Back to me and my schnoz. Yes, I know that it doesn’t really matter. But I also know that it kinda *does* matter. Because no matter how many people tell you that it's what's on the inside that counts, the hard, cold truth is that people do judge you by your looks. At least to begin with, anyway. Humans are shallow. That's just a fact. So we might as well get used to it.

After Mum and Dad split, my life was thrown into turmoil. It felt awful.

Imagine you're cruising on a calm, steady boat along the French Riviera ... gentle breeze wafting over you ... sun kissing your cheeks ... the sound of waves slowly sending you into a trance ...

... then suddenly you're in a giant industrial washing machine, set on not-delicate, heavy-duty, maximum spin. Your head banging against the sides of the tumbler, soap suds getting in your mouth – you have no idea how you got teleported into this mess and you're scrambling to get out.

That's basically what divorce feels like.

A tale of two suburbs

So now I have two lives. Monday to Thursday I live in the snooty eastern suburbs with Mum and her geriatric new husband, Patrick. I call him Plastic Pat because . . . how shall I put it? Well, he's had some 'work done'. That's adult speak for 'plastic surgery'.

Plastic surgery
Noun
(doesn't involve actual plastic)
When you voluntarily ask a doctor (with a scalpel) to rearrange your face/body through painful and expensive surgery!

He's 15 years older than Mum and trying to look young. So he's had the works.

CHIN TUCK.
NOSE NIP.
EAR FOLD.
EYE STRETCH.
BROW BOOST.
NECK CRIMP.
BELLY CROP.
BUTT LIFT.

YOU NAME IT,
HE'S DONE IT.

As a result, he looks . . .

Stretchy.

Pointy.

Plastic.

Hence Plastic Pat.

What I don't understand is why Mum, who spends her whole life telling me looks don't matter, went and married a guy who cares SO much about his looks. It makes no sense. But adults don't always make sense. I learnt that ages ago.

Patrick's favourite companion is his pocket mirror. I don't even think he knows Mum has a daughter.

ME!

I mean, yeah, sure, he's seen me around the house and occasionally he attempts small talk. He tries to act hip and young by saying random things like:

'Hey, TGIF, am I right?'

So cringey! I do the awkward nod and force a smile - and wonder to myself if his surgeon removed some vital parts of his brain during one of his nip and tuck operations.

But for real - he has not fully registered who I am. Maybe he figures he doesn't really have to bother. I'll be dead in a year anyway.

DEATH.

It always comes back to that. Sorry to bring it up again. It's just that it's hard to not think of dying when you're dying. It kind of casts a shadow over everything.

OR SHINES A LIGHT.

Depends how you look at it. I don't really see it as a dark, ominous thing. I mean, I did at first, but not so much anymore. It's been a little while since I found out and I guess I've adjusted to the idea . . . a bit. It's amazing how the human mind can shift its way of thinking. Its way of looking at the world. Like when you've been in the dark so long that you start to see. It's weird – at first you squint, but then your eyes adapt and you start to recognise shapes, objects, then if you stay there long enough, you'll even start to see detail.

We all know that life ends. That's a fact. But most of us don't think about that. Until we're forced to – like me. Then, suddenly an ordinary day in an ordinary life becomes extraordinary. You become 'the girl who's dying' and the way you see the world changes.

I'm not afraid of death.

Though I'll admit, when they first told me that *death* was just over there, around the corner, behind that yellow line, waiting for me, I was terrified. Completely shook. Totally freaked out. To my very core. But that feeling didn't last. The human brain is a curious and clever thing. It protects you like a lioness protects her cubs. She won't let you live in a permanent state of fear. So, after a while, I stopped being spooked by death. Me and the big D have come to terms with each other. Sometimes I even look forward to it. Not in an emo, morbid way or because I don't like my life. I'm just curious. Haven't you ever wondered what's on the other side?

Everyone has different views on that. And everyone thinks their view is the right one.

Mum is a believer. She's one thousand percent sure that there's an afterlife. And she's not just saying that to make me feel better. She's believed this ever since I can remember. She thinks it'd be foolish to think that this earthly life is all there is.

'Of course there's more to existence than just this! When you were a baby, growing inside my tummy, did you think it remotely possible that there would be a big, beautiful world like this outside the womb?'

'Um, not sure that I was having those big, existential thoughts when I was in your belly, Mum.'

'Of course you weren't! You were too busy growing – getting ready to come out and live your best life here.'

Live your best life – Mum's favourite mantra. Comes from too many self-help books and way too many episodes of *Oprah* when she was younger.

But I don't disagree with her 'life after life' theory. I mean, nobody really knows for sure, but I like the thought that there are worlds beyond this one . . . just life in different forms. Kind of like the different levels in *Super Mario Bros.* My fave game. #oldskool

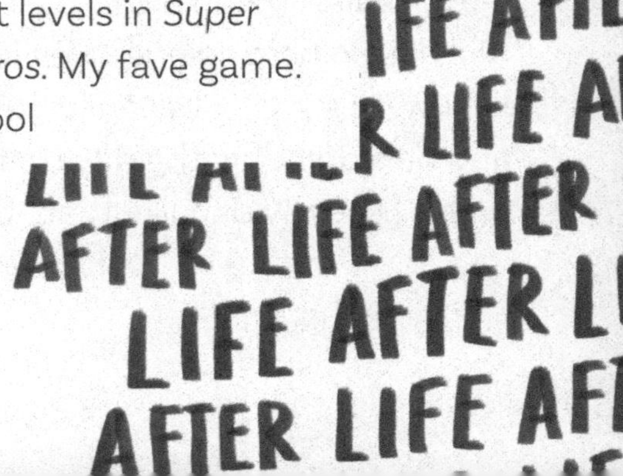

Dad

And then there's Dad. I live with him Fridays to Sundays. In the not-so-snooty western suburbs. Dad is definitely NOT a believer. I remember when I was little he and Mum often disagreed about the big-picture stuff.

'You get one shot at this life and then it's over. Finished. Lights out. Kaput.'

He's **two thousand percent** sure that there's no life after this one. You go six feet under and get eaten by worms. But he tries to make me feel better about dying by saying things like, 'Who'd want another wretched life anyway, Petal? I'd trade places with you in a heartbeat!'

And he says that because this whole situation is breaking his heart. I've seen him cry when he thinks I'm not around. And I don't mean just a whimper and a few tears. I mean a big, loud, ugly cry. Sometimes he cries so hard that it turns into a coughing fit. And I know he's crying because he's missing me already and he's dreading the day that I go. I feel sad too. When I see my dad like that, it's crippling. Feels like

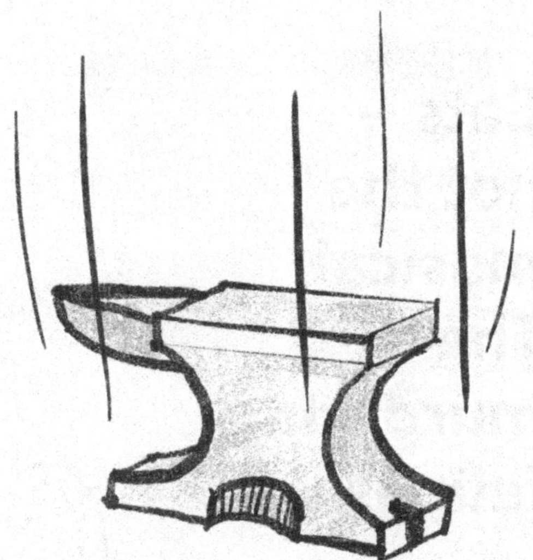

a big heavy anvil (like the ones in those Road Runner cartoons) landing on your chest.

How are he and Mum going to cope when I'm gone? Who's going to look after them? I'm not as sad for me. Of course I'll miss them like crazy, but I'm pretty sure Mum's right about there being an afterlife. I reckon I'll see them both again.

Over there.

On the other side.

In Level 2 of the game we call 'Life'.

Back to Dad, and his crazy household. Oh, I didn't mention that?

Yep, he's married to a woman called Wanda. Who came as a package deal with her **273** children. Okay, so I'm exaggerating. But not by much. She has three sons (Cash, Buzz and Dillon), two daughters (Brooke and Destiny), two dogs (Kim and Kanye) and one evil cat – Spanx.

Cats – not the musical. The murdering felines.

Can we just change the subject for a moment and talk about how evil cats are?

Let's face it, they're the Voldemort of the animal kingdom. You should see Spanx – he prances around like he's some big boss CEO, peeing wherever he wants and treating us all like his servants.

Have you ever had a death stare from a cat? That prickly 'I'm-about-to-scratch-your-eyes-

out' type of stare? It's terrifying. One evil look from a cat can burn a hole into your very soul.

Also, they KILL FOR FUN. Not for food, like all other carnivorous animals.

Just for funsies.

Cute, right?

And they like to torture their prey during the kill. Poke, prod, slice and dice and prolong the process, making the poor creature's death as hideous as possible.

So, in conclusion: they are not adorable fluffy furballs. They are diabolical murdering monsters. It's no wonder they're a witch's favourite pet!

Wanda

Wanda is salty.

> **Salty (*sawl*-tee)**
> *Adjective*
> **The state of being annoyed, irritated, peeved or cut. Triggered by life and everyone in it. That feeling of wishing you could press 'blast-off' on the jet-pack of your life, shoot off into space and not have to encounter another pesky human ever again.**

Wanda is salty about her failed career as a high-school science teacher. She just couldn't cope with any more badly behaved Year 9 boys. One time this obnoxious kid, Billy Kosta, bugged her so much that she threw a shoe at him in class. A stiletto. And she got him. Hole in one. Like a sniper. Her heel slashed his forehead. Right above his left eyebrow. He had to get six stitches. He had it coming, but needless to say, she lost her job.

She's also salty about the existence of hipsters.

'A bunch of bearded idiots with twirly moustaches and skinny jeans who do nothing but take pics of their lavender, turmeric lattes for their Instagram pages!'

She once ordered a hot chocolate when we were in hipster territory (closer to Mum's neighbourhood) and she got a cup of warm milk with two squares of Cadbury Dairy Milk on the side. It was called a 'deconstructed cream'o'cacao'.

She was **FURIOUS!**

She's salty about the price of loo paper these days. It can get expensive when there are eight butts to wipe in one household. But most of all, she's salty about having a hundred kids. Sometimes, she looks at them like she can't quite believe they're all hers. And not in a loving 'look-at-my-precious-children, I'm-so-blessed' kind of way. But in an 'OMG, is-this-really-my-life? How-did-I-end-up-here-with-all-these-rug-rats! Anyone-got-a-sledgehammer?' kind of way.

But I like her. She has a good heart and there's no pretending with her. What you see is what you get. And even though she's rough and run off her feet and almost always salty, she still finds the time to check in with me. Making sure I'm okay. Giving me a kiss on the forehead and squeezing me till my guts feel like they're going to pop out.

My bestie – Al

Al and I are besties. The bestest of all besties in all of Bestie Town. His full name is actually Alexander Aaron Afu but everyone calls him Al. Honestly, I don't know what I'd do without him in my life. And before you get all mushy about it, no, he's not my boyfriend. I mean, he's my friend and he's a boy, but we're not a thing. Al is the only person at school who knows about my illness. I've sworn him to absolute secrecy and he's been brilliant – like a vault – hasn't slipped up even once! He's trustworthy like that. Except he does do this one annoying thing – he just can't stop asking me questions about it.

'What's the name of the illness again?'
'Non-Hodgkin's lymphoma.'

'And that's the bad one, right? Hodgkin's is better than Non-Hodgkin's, am I right?'
'Al, all cancers are bad, but yes, I guess Hodgkin's has a better prognosis than what I've got.'

'Why didn't they just give it another name then? Why call it a "non" cancer when it's actually worse than the original?'

I wish you could have seen the look of genuine bewilderment on Al's face as he pondered this question. Like he'd just smelt an eggy fart and was trying to find the source. But just to put things in context, I should mention that Al is a curious kid generally. He can't help it. When he's not asking me questions about my cancer, he asks me a thousand other unanswerable questions.

'Why would it ever rain cats and dogs anyway? That's what I want to know.'

'It's just an expression, Al.'

'Well, it's stupid.'

'And why does the moon sometimes show up in the middle of the day?'

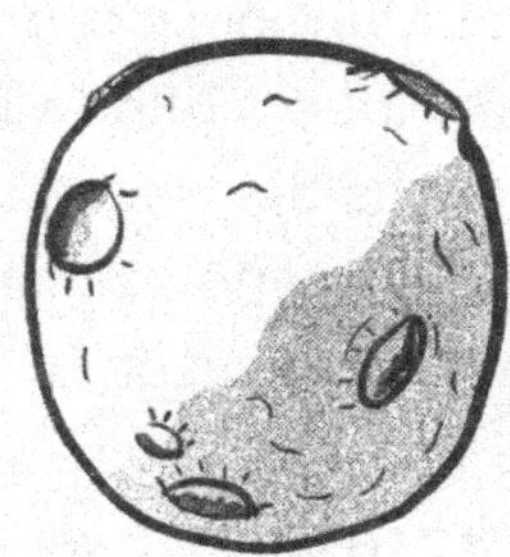

'Why does an echo echo echo echo echo echo echo echo echo?'

'And where do hiccups come from?'

'Which came first, the bacon or the egg?'

'Why don't humans have tails?'

'Have you ever tried licking your elbow? It's impossible. Go on, try it!'

I bet you just tried it – am I right?

☐ YES ☐ NO

Al has that effect on people. He always makes me think. And question. Why, **why**, **why?** It'd be easy to think 'why' about the cancer. Why now? Why me? Why not Alyssa Anderson, who is the personification of evil?

When I first got sick, I didn't want to believe it. I asked 'why' all the time. Nobody had any answers. Not Mum or Dad, or the doctors. Not even Spanx, the villainous, all-knowing cat. No one knew why things were as they were. They just were.

So I try not to ask why. Sometimes there's no rhyme or reason to life. Sometimes you just have to accept things as they are. Sometimes you have to think . . . well, why NOT?

Once I stopped looking for answers and just accepted it, life got a whole lot easier. The thing is, we're all going to die. The only thing that separates you from me is that I have a time frame to my life and yours is open-ended. Truth is, it could be tomorrow for you or next Thursday or in 77 years. You don't think about dying because you don't know when it's going to happen. I think about it because I know.

Alyssa – nemesis

Nemesis (*nem*-uh-sis)
Noun
A long-standing rival; an arch enemy, a foe, someone who makes your life so hellish that you'd rather listen to the *Frozen* soundtrack on loop for the rest of your life than have to deal with her ever again.

So, here we are. Full circle. I tried putting off the inevitable of having to tell you about Alyssa Anderson. But unfortunately she's an integral part of this story of the last year of my life – so there's no escaping her.

Butt Breath

She has a juicy wart on the tip of her nose. Occasionally it oozes pus.

Her feet are like lead. As in the heavy metal that bullets are made of. She doesn't walk, she stomps. You can hear her coming from a suburb away.

She roars like a lion.

RRRREEEOOOOOAAAARRRR!

And laughs like a hyena.

She has the morals and conscience of a flea.

And she eats small children for breakfast every morning.

Okay, so not all of that is entirely true. But some of it is. Maybe.

Unfortunately, what's actually **three thousand percent** true is this:

Alyssa Anderson is pretty, softly spoken and popular. Which is super confusing because her outside just doesn't match her inside. How can those piercing baby blue eyes shoot such greasy looks across the classroom?

How is it that out of her perfectly pouty lips come

such mean words? And green gooey spit that is targeted at me as I get off the bus every day?

And her hair . . . her beautiful, shiny, long blonde hair mocks me every time she flicks it with the back of her hand after she's said something nasty.

Yesterday she asked me if I was going to try out for the school play.

'It's a cracker this year,' she said. *Beauty and the Beast*. She said there'd be a part in there that I'd be perfect for.

The beast.

'Great role, and you wouldn't even need a costume . . . or make-up . . . or hair.'

I felt the lump in my throat get bigger as she was talking. And a sinking, sick feeling as I realised that there were other people within earshot. How humiliating. I should be used to Alyssa's cutting comments by now but I don't think meanness is something you can ever get used to.

'Definitely not hair. You've already got all that lovely body fur.' She then reached over and stroked my arm. 'So nice. Like a fluffy Persian carpet.'

She always finds a way to throw in something insulting about the fact that I'm half Persian.

Persian vs Iranian

I tell people I'm half Persian instead of half Iranian, even though technically speaking Iranian is more correct. Iran used to be called Persia but a lot of Iranians prefer to be called Persian because frankly, let's face it, it sounds better. Friendlier. More 'exotic'. More likely to be confused with 'Parisian'.

Suddenly you're thinking about croissants and the Eiffel Tower instead of nuclear bombs. Iran conjures up images of crazy ayatollahs and weapons of mass destruction.

Unfortunately, Middle Easterners have an image problem in the West. I'm actually proud of my Iranian heritage. The culture, the history, the food. It's all amazing. Ever since I can remember, my mum has talked about Iran with such love and longing. One of the oldest, most influential cultures in the world. Cyrus the Great (you must've heard of him) kicked it off. The great Persian Empire. For thousands of years, they led the way, whether it was through art, architecture, science, medicine or poetry. The Persians had it covered. We're not just about rugs and cats, you know. I hope in the next year, before I leave this planet for good, I get to visit Iran – my mother's homeland.

Maybe one day things will change. Maybe one day there'll be peace in the Middle East and being Iranian won't make people think you're a terrorist. Until then, I'm going with Persian. Life's hard enough without having to prove to people that I don't have a hand grenade in my back pocket.

Queen Mean

Back to Alyssa. Let me make one thing clear. I'm not overreacting. Or exaggerating. Or being a drama queen. Alyssa has picked on me repeatedly, consistently and unrelentingly since I moved schools in Year 5. Here are just a few of the things she's done to me over the years – in no particular order.

- Left a peanut butter sandwich in my locker with a note on it that said EAT ME. I'm allergic to peanuts. As in anaphylactic, 'will-swell-up-like-a-balloon-and-stop-breathing' allergic.
- Called me names like:

x GONZO → THAT CHARACTER FROM THE MUPPET SHOW WITH LARGE HOOKED NOSE

x FREAK

x LOSER

x GRONK

x SNITCH

x SNOT-RAG

x WEASEL

x MOOK

x FATTY BOOMBA (I HAVE CURVES LIKE AN ACTUAL HUMAN GIRL)

- Volunteered to give me a 'tour of the school' on my first day in Year 5 and took me straight to the 'Buddy Bench'. I was so happy. Did this mean we would be buddies? And we'd sit on this bench together?

Turns out, NO. This was the bench where losers like me, losers with no mates, can sit at lunchtime and wait for someone to take pity on them.

Then there's the spitting. Happens every day as I get off the bus. Most days I manage to dodge it. I've become a very fast runner. But some days,

SPLAt.

A gooey, green booger gets me right in the back. It's particularly bad if it lands in my hair. So gross. I have to shower as soon as I get home.

So, you get the picture. I'm not making things bigger than they are. It's not a one-off case of meanness or spite or two kids just not getting along. It's a textbook case of bullying. Repeated, ongoing, tyrannical oppression. Big words, I know. Look 'em up. They totally apply in this situation.

But here's some good news. All of that is about to change. Queen Mean Alyssa is about to hit an all-time low because tomorrow we're telling the school about my illness. She's going to realise that she's been bullying a dying girl and that is going to make her feel smaller than an ant, grubbier than a cockroach and slimier than a snake!

SPOT THE ANT ↓

Mum and Dad thought it was time to let the school know what was going on because soon I'll be missing classes to get treatment and I'll start looking sick and, I guess, because eventually you just have to let people know.

At first I didn't want to tell anyone because people are weird and totally awkward about sickness and death. They all react so differently. Some tilt their head to the side and look at you like you've suddenly turned into some kind of **TWO-HEADED PURPLE ALIEN**. Some well up with tears. Others straight-up cry. Some people try to act upbeat and positive and immediately tell you about all the different kinds of medical treatments that are available now and how science is progressing so everything is going to be fine. Then there are the alternative therapy types. If I just balance on my left foot every night at midnight, while facing the North Star and drink a kale, kombucha and snot combo juice, then my cancer will disappear. Like smoke into thin air.

Poof!

Other people just listen. Say nothing. You can see all their thoughts crashing into each other in their heads. Their faces say so much.

I wonder what Alyssa will do. For years I've wished I could say or do something to make her feel as bad as she makes me feel. But I've never been capable. I'm such a wuss at the whole mean-girl thing. But I think I've finally found my moment . . . shame it has to be at the expense of me DYING!

Here's how I think things are going to unfold when she finds out:

She's going to fall to her knees and beg for forgiveness.

The guilt.

Oh, the guilt.

The horrible, overwhelming guilt of it all.

She'll remember all the nasty things she's said and done to me over the years and it will hit her like a ton of bricks.

There will be tears. Projectile tears. Enough to fill a thousand buckets. She'll cry me a river, people. You hear? Alyssa Anderson is finally going to feel the full force of her actions and she will weep like a baby.

I'll let her squirm and grovel for a while but will ultimately forgive her because I'm the bigger person. But she won't be able to forgive herself. She'll try to make it up to me in whatever time I have left, so I'll let her . . .

polish my shoes . . .

carry my books . . .

pay for my lunches . . .

and pull me in a rickshaw all the way home on days when I don't feel like catching the bus. I'll insist she goes especially fast up that mega hill leading to my house.

I'll have everything on the menu. Times two. Make that three. I'll have three of absolutely everything on the menu. Except for the bucket of BBQ chicken wings. I'll have four of those. I just love the marinade on those wings. So tasty.

Do you think that's a reasonable prediction of how things are going to unfold tomorrow? I guess we'll know soon enough. Only one more sleep until . . .

D-Day*

I wake up with knots in my belly. I bolt up in bed. My heart is racing. My palms are sweaty. Is this part of my sickness or am I just nervous about officially becoming the 'Cancer Girl' at school? I notice that Mum is lying next to me. This isn't unusual. Since my diagnosis, she often curls up in my bed and cuddles me through the night. It's comforting.

Panic sets in. I'm breathing but I can't seem to inhale enough oxygen. Mum wakes up and takes my hand.

'Are you okay, sweetheart?'

I don't want to worry her but I can't lie. I've never been able to lie. It's a curse.

I tell her that I don't want to do this.

That I don't want to tell the school.

That I don't want it to be true.

That I don't want to die.

She listens. And strokes my hand. And tells me that I don't have to do anything I don't want to do. Then I start crying. Today I don't feel strong. Suddenly I don't care about Alyssa or how bad she's going to feel. And I don't care that there's an afterlife. I don't want to go there.

**Generally refers to the day on which any large-scale operation is planned to start.*

I want to stay here.

In this life.

With Mum and Dad. And Al and Wanda and my 273 step-siblings. I want to awkwardly navigate my way through the icky teenage years and come out the other side. I want to listen to cringey songs and dye my hair pink. I want to fall in love. And go to a music festival. And learn how to make dumplings. Not necessarily in that order.

I want to grow up. I want to grow old.

I want to live.

I cry and I cry and I cry. Buckets. And so does Mum. We cry and talk and hold each other till neither of us can cry anymore. Then, just as she's telling me that she's going to ring the school and tell them that we're not going in today, I change my mind. 'It's okay, Mum. I can do it.' Mum squeezes my hand. 'There is no rush, sweetie. Your school can wait. Your dad and I can wait. Everybody can wait.'

'Stop the world, I want to get off!' I say melodramatically.

'Exactly,' says Mum. 'We are going to do this on *your* timeline. When *you're* ready.'

I tell her that I *am* ready. Somehow, all that crying has made me feel better. I mean, sure, it was exhausting. Crying, proper crying, is tiring work. Like running an emotional marathon. But for some reason, once I reached the finish line, I felt strong.

Energised, even. It was cathartic.

> **Cathartic (kath-*ah*-tik)**
> *Adjective*
> The process of releasing a sudden flood of emotions through a particular activity – it might be howling at the moon, smashing plates at a Greek wedding or crying with your mama till you're all cried out.

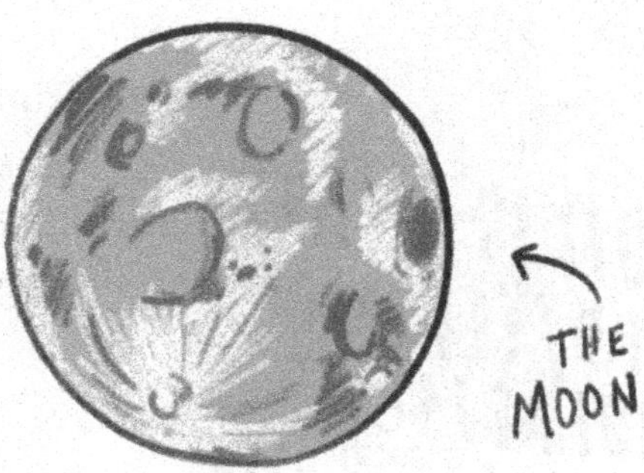

As I'm about to leap out of bed, Plastic Pat pokes his head around the door. He's holding two cups of tea. His face is puffy, like he's been crying too. Of course it's probably swollen from too much Botox but it's still sweet of him to bring us a cuppa.

Mum wipes my tears and kisses my face. She tries one more time to give me an out.

'Why don't we blow off school and do something fun today? Somebody say BOOKSTORE?'

Mum and I are nerdy like that. There's nothing we love doing more than hitting the bookstores, perusing books for hours, inhaling that 'book smell' and buying a stack of new reads. I feel smarter just by being near books - as if all that knowledge and all those perfectly woven words are entering my system through osmosis.

But not today. Today is D-Day. And I am ready. It's time.

'Okay, Ana joon, if you say so,' says Mum.

'I do!' I say as I jump out of bed and start getting ready. 'Now, come on. Let's go!'

JOON IS A FARSI WORD/TERM OF ENDEARMENT WHICH LITERALLY MEANS 'LIFE' BUT IS INTERCHANGEABLE FOR 'DEAR', 'DARLING' OR 'MY PRECIOUS LITTLE BAKLAVA'.

Let's do this

Dad meets us at school. He must've arrived super early because he looks tired and he tells us he's already on his third cup of coffee. We meet at the gate. He and Mum hug hello. It's weird how well they've been getting along since I got sick. After all those years of arguing and bickering and avoiding each other like the plague, they're now suddenly best buds. Shame it took me dying to bring them together like this.

'So how do you want to do this, Petal?' asks Dad.

I tell him that there is only one way to do this:

Fearlessly.

He laughs and hugs me extra tight.

'Lead the way, Ana Banana. Mum and I will follow.'

Truth is, I have no idea what I'm going to say once we get into the principal's office. I have no idea what fearlessness looks like. But something inside me just says: 'GO! Don't be afraid. Everything's going to be okay.'

And so I lead the way and confidently march towards Ms Longbottom's office.

Principal Longbottom

Oh, I probably should have told you about our principal before now. Her name is clearly distracting. And yet, somehow, because it's such an obviously ridiculous name, kids seem to not find it ridiculous. It's one of those absurd things. You'd think a school principal with a name like **Longbottom** would have a terrible time, but that's just not the case. Nobody blinks. We don't even find it funny. And when a new kid comes to the school and tries to get mileage out of her name, they're met with blank, bored stares. I totally get that this is weird. But it's just the way it is. There's also a boy in Year 9 called Jason Sidebottom. I kid you not. You can't make this stuff up. But no one finds his name funny either. He's just 'Jase' – the kid with the red hair. I imagine if there was anyone with the last name of *Front*bottom, then there'd be problems. But for now, we're clear.

Ms Longbottom welcomes us warmly into her room. The next 45 minutes are kind of a blur. Nothing seems linear. I am there but not there. I feel like I am falling through time.

Falling and falling . . .

I know that we told her about the Non-Hodgkin's. About my predicted life expectancy. She was particularly cranky at my doctor for putting a timeline on my life. Dad tried to explain that we pushed Dr Needham to tell us the harsh truth. That I could in fact live longer than a year. Or perhaps less. That it wasn't impossible for me to fully recover (because nothing's impossible) but that it was highly improbable. The grown-ups talked for a long time. I tuned in and out. As if I was surfing through channels looking for something better to watch.

My patchy memory of the conversation looks a little like this:

Ms Longbottom: Ana, I want you to know that I, personally, and the school, are here to support you through this journey in every way that we can.

Me: (Looking for the remote control to my brain.)

Ms Longbottom: We will make sure that everyone is fully on board . . .

Me: (Where's that damn remote?)

Ms Longbottom: . . . offer whatever love and support you need over the next few months and . . . blah, blah, blah . . .

Me: (Found it!! I found the remote! I frantically switch the channel.)

Dance break!

This is not just *any* dance break, people. It's an Irish dance break.

Can we just talk about Irish dancing for a moment? Those guys DON'T MOVE THEIR ARMS! It looks so un-co and weird. As if their torsos have been mummified and their legs are trying to break free.

And the costumes! What is going on there? It's like someone took to an Amish outfit with a sequin gun.

But the music is awesome. If you close your eyes right now, you can hear it. Go on, try it . . .

Isn't it cool? Well, maybe not conventionally 'cool' like you'd find under the 'popular' section in Spotify, but cool in a trippy Irish kind of way.

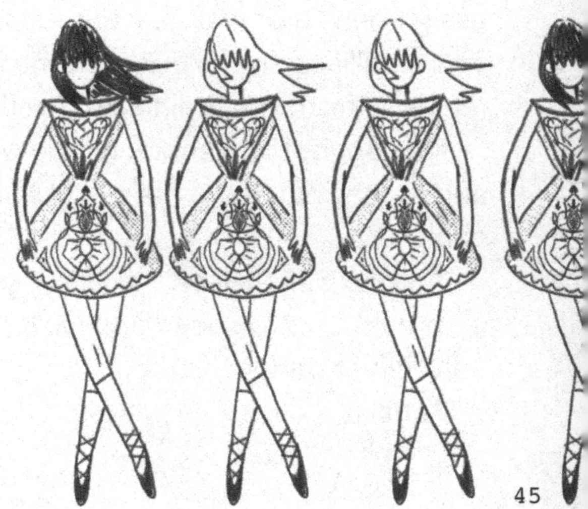

Back to Longbottom's office

As we were exiting Ms Longbottom's office, I realised that I'd been on a mental 'dance break' for almost the entire time. My brain has its own way of dealing with stressful situations. Today it took a 'dance break' but sometimes it checks out in other ways. Sometimes it goes time travelling like Doctor Who. That can get really interesting. When my parents were going through their divorce, my 'brain breaks' were in all kinds of incredible places. One time, during one of their fights, I went back in time and hung out with Albert Einstein. We talked about our shared love of cheese, his cranky hairdresser (who was the reason he swore off haircuts forever) and my science assignment that was due the following week. I got some brilliant one-on-one tutoring on the theory of relativity from the Brainiac himself.

Ms Longbottom shook hands with Mum and Dad and surprisingly gave me a hug. I half hugged her back.

'Ana, Mr Sahabdeen' – that's my year adviser – 'will be brought up to speed and we'll share the news before first period.'

Bam.

Done.

Just like that, the news was out. There was no taking it back now. The principal knew and before long, the whole school would know too.

Mum and Dad asked if I wanted to wag the day and go home but I said no. There was no point putting this off. Might as well face the music now. I said goodbye to my parents and messaged Al. He was on the bus, on his way to school. I was desperate to see him so I waited for him at the gate.

Once he arrived, I told him all about our meeting with Longbottom and how I had totally spaced out during the chat, and that all I knew was that in less than 20 minutes, everyone – including Butt Breath Anderson – would know that I'm dying.

Al put his arm around me and reassured me that it was all going to be fine. He even managed to make me laugh. Not about what was going to happen but about an incident on the bus. Something to do with Louis Finley (a Year 10 thug) trying to light his fart with a match and it going horribly wrong. Quite literally a 'pants-on-fire' situation.

QUESTION:

DO BOYS EVER STOP FINDING FARTS FUNNY?

Actually, don't answer that. My dad still cracks up at the very mention of any kind of flatulence – be it silent, deadly, loud or proud.

Silence fell upon the land

Picture tumbleweed blowing along the school corridors. Not a sound to be heard anywhere. Just stunned, ashen-faced kids walking to their classes in silence. Okay, so I exaggerate, but that's what it felt like after everyone heard the news. There were no tilted heads saying how sorry they were. No tears. Not even any questions. Mr Sahabdeen told my entire year that I AM DYING and nothing. Just silence. Deafening silence. Al says it's shock. People freeze when they're in shock. They don't know what to say so they don't say anything. So what we had then was a major case of awks.

Awks
(short for awkward - not an actual word)
Adjective
When something causes an uneasy, embarrassing feeling. Like saying a big, long goodbye to someone on the street then realising you're walking in the same direction. Or madly waving at someone you know, but it's not actually them. Or that time when my dad went through Macca's drive-through and started placing his order and the lady shouted, 'Can you drive to the speaker? You're talking into the rubbish bin!'

Super awkward silent kids walked off to their various classes. I didn't know where to look. Or what to do. Thank God for Al. He made up for all the silence by talking nonstop. It's called overcompensating. He barely stopped to catch his breath. At one point I thought he was actually going to choke on his own words.

Al: 'What have you got now? I've got Science. With Ms Punch. Last lesson we learnt that animals can rain from the sky. For real. Actual phenomenal scientific fact. Can you believe it? Animals falling from the sky in a rainfall. Fish and frogs are the most common, with birds coming third. Can you imagine walking down the street, then *THUD*, you're hit on the noggin by a stinky falling fish? It's absurd. Yet true. Remarkable, really. Hey, so maybe "raining cats and dogs" isn't just an expression after all?'

He went on and on . . .

'How hungry are you right now? On a scale of one to ten? I'm like an eleven. Seriously. I could eat a horse! That's another stupid expression, don't you think? I mean, who can eat an ACTUAL horse? Although . . . maybe if I hadn't eaten in weeks and the horse was tender and juicy . . . maybe then I could. I'd definitely need hot sauce though.'

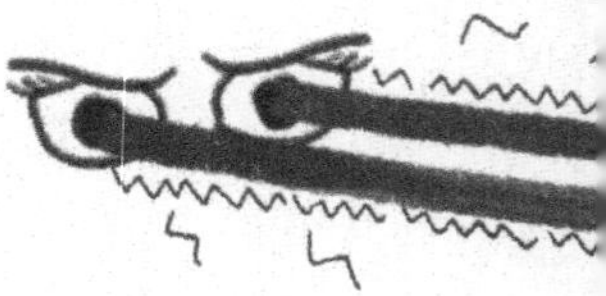

. . . and on and . . .

on and ...

I started to tune out and soon his voice just became white noise. Distorted and distant. All I could think was – why wasn't anyone reacting? Didn't anyone care? I really thought this moment would be epic. A turning point. Not a non-event.

And then it happened. The most surreal thing ever. From the corner of my eye, I felt the weight of her nasty glare. Her stares were like laser beams. I could feel the heat of it on my shoulder – almost like it was about to burn a hole into my polyester hoodie.

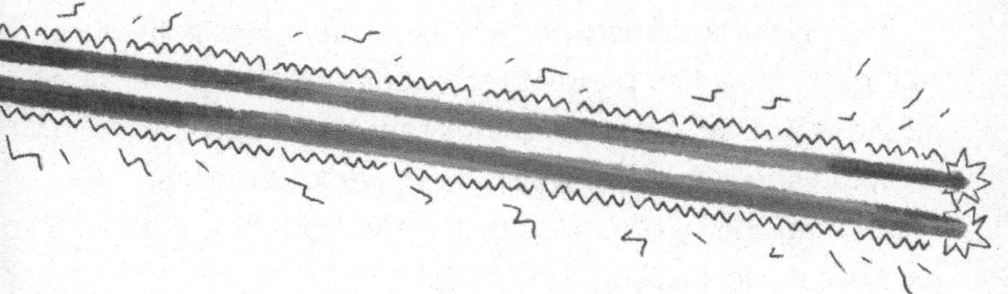

Al suddenly stopped talking and tugged on my arm. He twisted my sleeve into a knot as he whispered into my ear, 'Oh, em, gee Ana . . . it's her! HER! And she's making a beeline for you!'

Time seemed to stand still for a moment. Like a vignette. A frozen picture. The only movement was Alyssa walking towards me. She got closer and closer. In slow motion. The sound of her footsteps pounding into my brain, unnaturally loud, almost bursting my eardrums.

THUD. THUD. THUD.

The long silence was about to be broken. Someone was finally going to acknowledge the news of my illness. My imminent death. And it was going to be Butt Breath. Kinda perfect, I thought. Was she going to come good? Just as I had imagined? Are we up to the 'shoe polishing' part of the story yet?

I took a deep breath.

I turned to face the beast.

And there she was.

Alyssa. Anderson.

Looking ridiculously perfect, as always. Her golden hair glistening. Her pearly teeth beaming, **ding!** Her lip gloss just so. A million things raced through my mind as she made her way over to me but before I could catch my breath or order my thoughts, she was upon me. Smiling. SMILING!

'Hey, Ana . . .'

She'd never called me by my name before. Lately she'd been calling me 'Porkie'.

'I'm really sorry about what's happening to you.'

Al and I exchanged looks. We had officially entered the Twilight Zone.

'And I'm sorry I've been such a cow to you for so long.'

I went to open my mouth and say something but no words came out. I should have prepared myself better for this moment. Like when award nominees have an acceptance speech ready. Just in case.

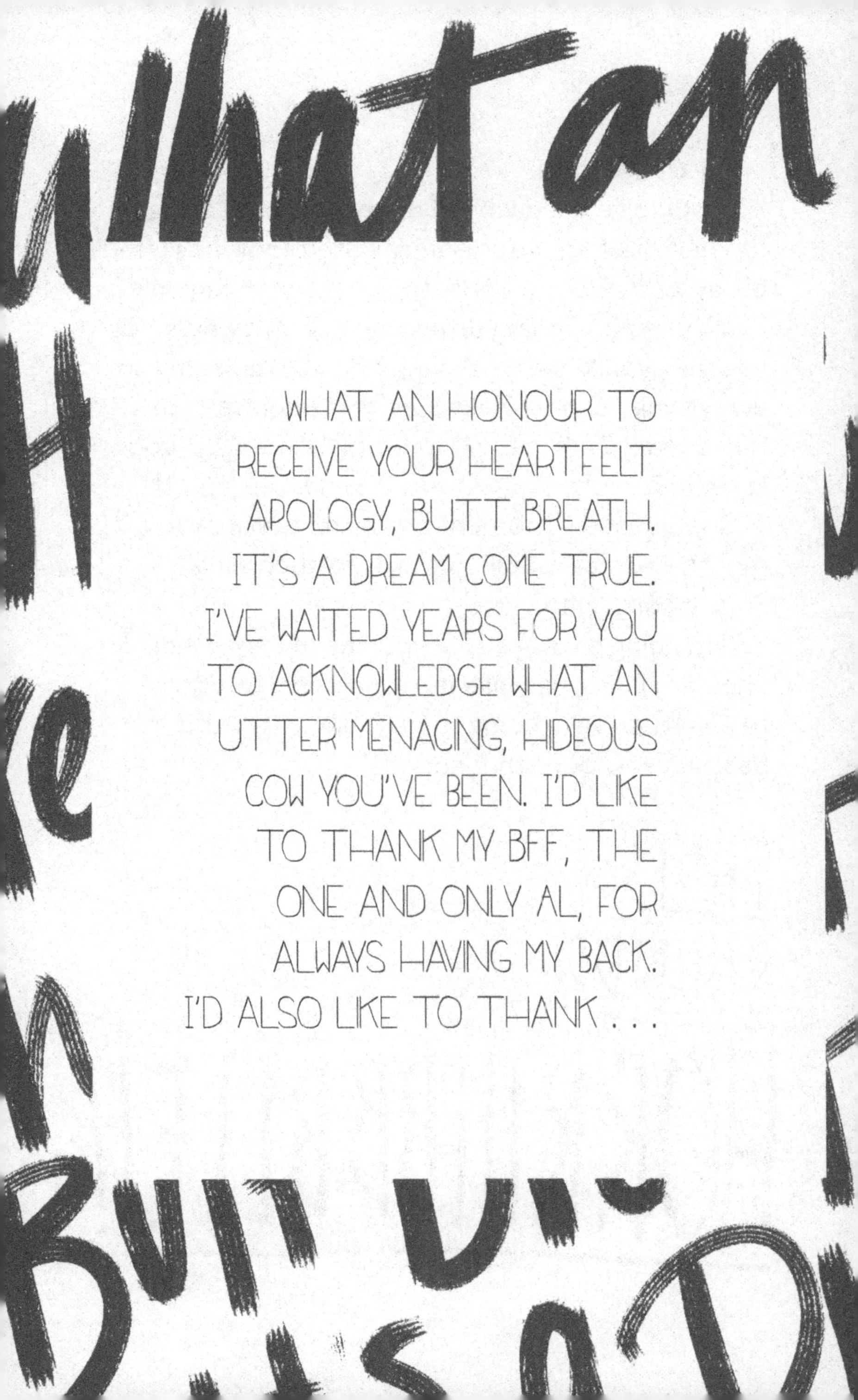

WHAT AN HONOUR TO RECEIVE YOUR HEARTFELT APOLOGY, BUTT BREATH. IT'S A DREAM COME TRUE. I'VE WAITED YEARS FOR YOU TO ACKNOWLEDGE WHAT AN UTTER MENACING, HIDEOUS COW YOU'VE BEEN. I'D LIKE TO THANK MY BFF, THE ONE AND ONLY AL, FOR ALWAYS HAVING MY BACK. I'D ALSO LIKE TO THANK . . .

Alyssa went on.

'I would've cried when Sahabdeen was telling us the news but I'm not wearing waterproof mascara today. And nobody wants to see me with big ugly black streaks running down my face. Anyway, since you're . . . you know . . . moving on . . . I'm going to do everything I can to make sure that your last year . . . Is it a year? Or months? How long before you, you know . . . ?'

She paused a moment for my response. My mouth was open. Still no words forthcoming. So she continued.

'I'm going to make sure your last days are happy ones. I'm going to make it my personal business to see to it. We're going to be friends, you and me. Besties. How does that sound?'

THAT

SOUNDS

HORRIIIBBBLLE!!

You ever had one of those terrifying dreams when you're trying to SCREAM but no matter how hard you try, your voice just won't come out?

Look, I know I fantasised about Alyssa repenting and becoming my personal shoe-shining servant but now that we're here, I TAKE IT ALL BACK! The only thing worse than Alyssa Anderson being nasty is Alyssa Anderson being nice. A kind and friendly Alyssa Anderson is like an angry and abusive Mary Poppins. No. Just no. Something about it isn't right. It's jarring. And deeply disturbing. I don't buy the 'nice' act. I wasn't born yesterday. She's up to something. Something sinister. Something dark. Something truly wicked.

But what?

Al (who was also dumbstruck and silent) was still twisting my jumper. He'd done about 13 rotations so my sleeve was all bunched up and cutting off circulation in my arm. I finally managed to close my gaping jaw.

GULP.

Alyssa told me that she knew this was a lot to take in. 'You're probably thinking, "What's she up to?" – am I right?'

All I could do was stare. Not even blink. Just stare at her in disbelief. Al, meanwhile, nodded furiously. So furiously that I was worried his head was going to dislodge and fly off his neck.

Alyssa continued. 'And doubting my intentions.'

Suddenly Al's motormouth kicked into gear. Before I knew it, he was all up in her face.

'Uh . . . yeah! SERIOUSLY doubting your intentions right now. Who wouldn't? You've been nothing but mean, mean, mean to Ana since forever and now, out of nowhere, you want to be besties? I'm sorry. It's not gonna happen. Besides, the position of Bestie is already taken.'

Alyssa laughed at Al in a super patronising way, then looked away and continued to talk to me. 'Aw, cute, I didn't realise he was your spokesperson. Or is he your agent? So adorbs.'

Al's nostrils flared. He was *not* happy. Alyssa continued.

'Anyway, don't be suss, Ana. Even though you have every reason to be. This is legit. I want us to be friends. I want to make it up to you. And I'm really, truly sorry for being such a ...' She trailed off, trying to think of the right word. For a moment, she seemed humble and a bit ashamed. She looked at the ground. Al and I looked at each other in utter disbelief. Was it possible that we were, perhaps, witnessing a genuine apology?! Alyssa finally found the word she was looking for.

' . . . #*%@#!'

Al's face looked like that shocked yellow emoji with the round googly eyes. Alyssa 'Butt Breath' Anderson had just apologised for being a cow again. Except this time she didn't say 'cow' – she used another word starting with 'b' which I'm not allowed to repeat in print – but a word that I think describes her perfectly.

Kim and Kanye (Woof)

I'd never been happier to see those two stinky mutts than I was that day. After dealing with so many humans on such a heavy day, I was delighted to come home to a couple of overenthusiastic, non-judgey, happy-go-lucky, butt-sniffing dogs. I swear animals are the best living creatures on this planet.

Don't get excited.

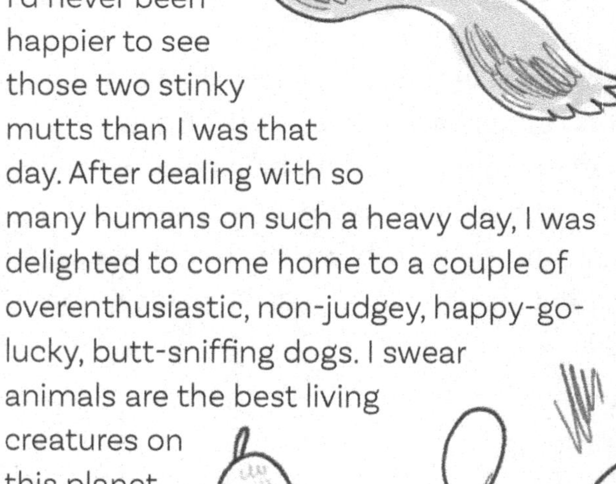

I still hate cats. Nothing will ever change that.

Wanda was in top form. She'd plonked the 273 sibs in front of the TV and given them hard candy to chew on. It's what she does when she wants complete quiet. The combination of TV plus rock sugar means that the kids don't move or talk for a serious amount of time. What happens afterwards is usually disastrous but sometimes Wanda resorts to this method in order to find a moment's peace. This was one of those times. She wanted quiet so that she could devote all her attention to me.

And here's the best thing about Wanda. Unlike other grown-ups who want to talk all the time and analyse things and ask you how you're feeling, she knows when to shut up. So instead of asking about my terrible day, she made us a huge bowl of popcorn and set up the beanbags in front of the second telly and introduced me to *Stand By Me* – an '80s movie classic about four 12-year-old boys who hear about a dead body in the woods, then set off on an adventure that shapes the rest of their lives. Neither of us said a word. We snuggled up with the dogs and with each other and watched one of the best movies I'd ever seen.

And for those two hours, everything in the world was just as it should have been.

Parallel universe

The next few weeks were a ridiculous game of cat and mouse. Alyssa being the cat (of course) and me, the mouse.

She just wouldn't leave me alone. At every turn, she was there, like a creepy clown in a horror flick.

In front of me in Maths class. Behind me in the canteen line. Next to me on the bus. Around every corridor. Smiling. Always smiling and wanting to 'chat'. Then there were the selfies. Every time Alyssa managed to corner me, she would take a selfie of us together. Urrgh!

Selfie mania

I'm afraid I have to change the subject again for a moment because there's no way I can mention selfies without my body contorting and going into a spasm and my left eye twitching like I'm some kind of deranged lunatic. The reason for this is that I HATE selfies. And the whole 'look-at-me' selfie culture. Yes, I know I probably sound like your out-of-touch 90-year-old nagging nana right now, but hear me out.

#nomakeupselfie
#iwokeuplikethis
#donthatemecozimbeautiful
#lookatmypout
#bluuuurrrgh

WHAT. IS. GOING. ON. PEOPLE?

A girl in my English class, Sasha Lalic, has literally thousands of embarrassing pouty selfies on her Insta page. One after another after another. I guess it'd be all right if she was actually doing something in some of the pics – like rollerskating or jumping out of a plane or even eating a burger, but nah . . . just endless poses. Different angles of her face and body. And if she doesn't get at least 100 'likes' within ten seconds of posting a pic, she goes into a total funk. Her pout becomes real. Her face sinks and her shoulders droop. She hides her phone under her desk during class and presses 'refresh' over and over again – ever hopeful for more 'likes'. She's a selfie junkie. It's her drug of choice. And she's not the only one. Half the kids in my year are caught up in it. Sometimes I think I'm an alien – with Al, my trusted goofy co-alien – in a selfie-obsessed world that just doesn't make sense.

Back to the Twilight Zone

The selfies that Alyssa takes of the two of us usually look something like this:

Why does she have to take a pic of every encounter?

Is she genuinely trying to make amends?

Does she really want to be friends?

Sometimes I start to think that maybe she's changed. Maybe I should give her the benefit of the doubt. Maybe me dying has made her think about things on another level.

Given her perspective.
Empathy, even.
Maybe she *is*
truly sorry.

Sharp focus

Focus is the basic rule of photography. Technically speaking, a good photo isn't blurry, dull or unclear. It's crisp, clear and sharp. With vibrant colours and good composition.

Why am I suddenly talking about photography? No, this isn't an unannounced 'brain break'. It's a metaphor, people.

> **Metaphor (*met*-uh-*fawr*)**
> *Noun*
> A figure of speech that describes one thing by comparing it to another. Like that Alicia Keys song 'Girl on Fire'. Clearly she isn't ACTUALLY on fire. 'Cause, you know, that would be bad. You'd have to whip out the fire extinguisher and go nuts on those flames before she ends up in the burns unit at the local hospital. No, this metaphor means that you'd better not mess with this girl. She's strong, she's independent, she is fearless. This queen can walk on fire, so you'd better watch out!

Back to my metaphor. We all look at life through our own particular lenses. Some people are optimists, glass half full, always seeing things through rose-coloured glasses. Sunshine and lollipops. And some people are pessimists, doom and gloom. Everything sucks and then you die.

I'm somewhere in the middle. I used to be a glass-half-full girl.

THEN I GOT CANCER.

Obviously that changed my perspective a bit. Now I swing from one side to the other. Sometimes I'm in the light, soaking up the sun and loving life sideways, and sometimes I hide in the shadows, bury my head under my pillow and cry into my mattress. But whichever way you look at life, things always seem a bit blurry.

Now I'm going to tell you something controversial. Cancer has a way of pulling things into sharp focus.

Cancer can be a gift.

Yes, cancer. The dreaded, horrible, life-sucking disease that nobody wants to get.

It's a gift that helps you see your life clearly.

Suddenly you can see what truly matters in a way that you'd never be able to if you weren't dying. I'm not saying this clarity is permanent. It comes and goes. But when you're facing the end, like I am, you start to see very clearly what REALLY matters in this world. And if I had to condense it down to just one word, it would be . . .

LOVE

You might think that's corny. But it's true. When you're in a face-off situation with the Grim Reaper, you realise that nothing in the world is more important than love. And I don't mean *luuurve*, as in sexy romantic love. **Eew**.

Although, that's legit too.

I mean love in all its different shapes and forms. Like when your mum declares a 'love bomb day' and makes it mandatory to skip school and only do things that you love.

Or the way your dogs bolt for the door and leap up for a hug the minute you step into the house.

Or when you look up at the night sky and realise that you're a tiny speck compared to the vast expanse of the universe and your lungs suddenly fill up – not with fear and freak-out but with awe and wonder.

Or when you help your little sister finally figure out long division and she's so happy, she literally starts doing cartwheels.

That's the sneaky thing about love. It comes in all kinds of different packages. Big, small, curly or straight. All-consuming and heavy like a boulder or sunny and light as a feather.

Love is the answer to just about every question you could ever think to ask.

Even one small kind act like Al lending a boofhead like Louis Finley his sports pants on the bus (and copping a detention for not bringing his sports gear to PDHPE) is a mighty act of love. And the effects of it ripple through the universe in a mystical, magical way.

Now, I should probably clarify something. With all this talk of love, don't be thinking I'm suddenly loving Butt Breath.

Hell, no.

I'm not a saint. Not yet, anyway.

I'm just realising that all the time and energy I spend thinking about her is wasted. What I should be doing instead is focusing on the people and things I do love. When you see the good in the world, that 'good' multiplies.

od good good good good good good good good g
od good good good good good good g
od good good good good good g
od good good good good good g
od good good good good g
ood good good good good g
ood good good good good g
ood good good good good g
ood good good good good g

And takes up more space, pushing the Butt Breaths in the world to the edges. But finding the good in the bad is an art form. Some people spend their entire lives trying to perfect it. Sometimes it requires a superhuman ability to home in on the tiniest pretty detail. Like finding a butterfly fluttering amid an enormous pile of garbage in a toxic landfill dumpster.

I'm killin' it with the metaphors today.

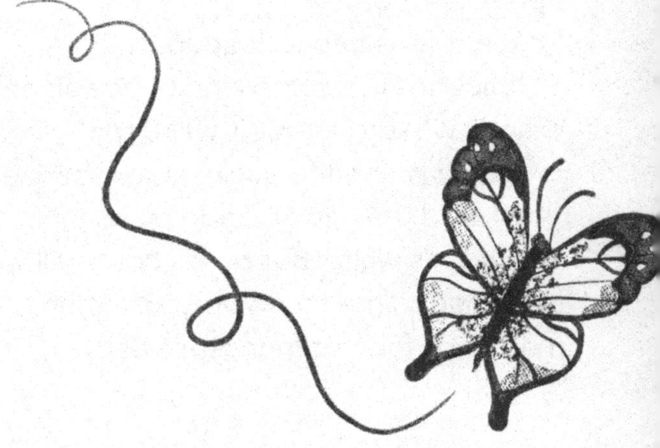

My butterfly

Her name is Ekua. She's the nurse who administers my chemotherapy every Tuesday. We first bonded over our names and the fact that no one EVER gets it right the first time.

Or the second.

Or the 277th time.

I thought that like 'Anahita', 'Ekua' would have some deep, mystical meaning too. 'Warrior Princess' perhaps, or 'Slay Queen', but it turns out 'Ekua' simply means 'born on a Wednesday'. And here's the kicker. Ekua was born on a Saturday!

I found all this out the very first time I was getting chemo. Let's just pause for a millisecond and talk about chemo.

Yes, it is as bad as it sounds.

It sounds like some kind of poison and that's exactly what it is. Isn't it weird that when your body is riddled with a life-sucking disease like cancer, that you'd then go and add poison into the mix? Yes, yes it's weird. But here's how it all works, as explained to me by my very scientific, matter-of-fact, no-nonsense dad.

IT'S A Good Cell *vs* Bad Cell SITUATION.

A battle. Imagine two cells entering a boxing ring. Each one has their coach. Rubbing their shoulders. Giving them inspirational pep talks.

'C'mon! You got this!'

'Float like a butterfly, sting like a bee!'

The crowd is excited. Supporters cheer. Fans holler. These two cells are ready for the battle of their lives. Well, for my life, actually. But before the ref has even rung the starting bell, the cancer cell throws the first punch.

Then the second and the third.

It goes nuts – kicking, scratching, pinching and spitting fireballs. Cheating like a beast.

Cancer cells have no manners. No respect for the rules. Those scumbags want world domination. And their world is my body. So they fight hard and they fight dirty. The Good Cell fights back as hard as it can but it's not a fair fight.

Now, imagine this fight not just between two cells but hundreds, thousands, maybe even a trillion cells. There's basically a mega battle between **good** and **evil** going on in my body.

That's where chemo comes in. When the bad guys are winning, chemotherapy is deployed as a weapon, to fight back and wipe those suckers out. Chemo does not muck around. It takes no prisoners. It's been brought in to annihilate and that is exactly what it does.

Now, you should know that some good cells get hurt in this process too. With all that poison being hurled at the bad cells, there are bound to be some casualties. That's what they call 'side effects'. But more on that later.

So that's 'Chemotherapy 101' as explained to me by Dad.

Got it?

Good.

Luckily, I am what they call an 'outpatient' for chemo, so I go in for day treatments and don't have to stay overnight. Dad took me in the first time. He was doing his part, being calm and comforting, holding my hand tight (a little *too* tight!) but I was still terrified. My heart beating a million miles a minute.

Hospitals, even children's hospitals, aren't kid-friendly places. There's so much equipment around. So much beeping and buzzing. People hooked up to machines, drips and tubes. Bags of wee hanging on the side of beds.

'You think that's Fanta?' whispered Dad, trying to lighten the mood. I threw him an unimpressed look but he was on a roll.

'Mountain Dew?'

I suppressed my gag reflex. 'Gross, Dad.'

And the smell of the place. How can I describe it? Unlike anything that's passed through these nostrils ever before. Like a combination of nail polish remover and bin juice. In short, hospitals are SERIOUSLY depressing places.

But in came Ekua with such warmth and ease. She had long braided hair tied up into a perfectly sculpted bun. Kind eyes and beautiful skin. And her smile was so big and infectious that you had no choice but to smile back. Even if you didn't feel like smiling, the muscles around your mouth would

SIDENOTE:
YAWNS AND SMILES ARE BOTH CONTAGIOUS.
FACTS

involuntarily curl up into a grin when she smiled at you.

Anyway, in she came and pretty much did a whole stand-up comedy routine for me about her name and all the grief it's given her in her life. I don't know how she did it, but she had me (and Dad) in stitches. I was laughing so hard and feeling so relaxed as she gently stuck a cannula into my veins and injected me with poison.

That is the magic of Ekua.

If it wasn't for her, my weekly hospital visits would be unbearable. But here's the trippy thing – I now actually look forward to Tuesday-drug-days. I do!

Every week she tells me a story about her life. Chronologically. Starting from when and where she was born up until today. We're currently about six chapters into her life. Childhood stories filled with so much fun and adventure. Sometimes I wonder if she's making half of it up just to keep me entertained. But it doesn't really matter. She's a great storyteller and she has me on the edge of my seat every week.

After that first day, she changed her roster to make sure she's working every single Tuesday so that she can treat me. And when I say 'treat', I mean she really treats me! I get some sort of rare, limited edition, imported candy every week. From Jolly Ranchers to Jujyfruits to Japanese green-tea Kit Kats. All kinds of explosive new flavours for my tastebuds. She also brings things to brighten the room. Flowers from her garden or a helium balloon, so she can inhale the gas and talk in a squeaky voice (which always makes me laugh). Once, she even brought in a *Stranger Things* poster 'cause she knows how much I love the show.

Ekua has a son. She skipped a few 'Life' chapters ahead, that's how I know this. She gave him a normal, bland and pronounceable name - John. But he doesn't live with her. He lives in Senegal with his dad. She misses him a lot, even though they speak every day.

As complicated as my life is, what with the cancer, my nemesis, Mum and Dad's complicated post-divorce arrangement, Pat, Wanda and the 273 step-sibs, Ekua's situation is even more complicated. Because she also has distance to deal with. And not just 40 minutes of annoying traffic which separates her and her son, but the Indian Ocean!

* (MAP NOT ENTIRELY CORRECT. COASTLINES ARE TRICKY.)

She works hard and sends almost all of her earnings back to Senegal for her son's education. It's fair to say she's serious about school, so when I told her about my upcoming exams, she changed gears and went into full mama-support mode. Making sure I knew that being sick didn't exempt me from trying my hardest. As far as she was concerned, even if the world was ending and we were witnessing the apocalypse in real time, there'd be no pause on the study button. You had to cram that knowledge in, even if you were doing it with your very last breath! Luckily for both of us, I agreed with her. So we didn't have a fight on our hands.

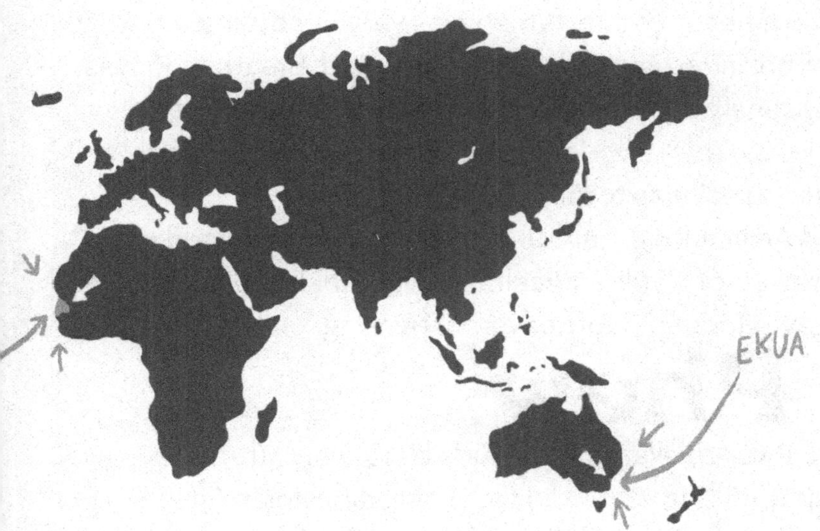

Exam season

Butt Breath was in top form during exam week. Still stalking me and trying to be 'nice'. Taking selfies at every turn. Offering to be my study buddy. AS IF! I'd rather eat toe jam than cram for exams with her. Of course, I didn't say that – 'cause I'm gutless like that. I just told her that I preferred studying on my own. I held my breath and waited for her response. Was she going to get offended and spew out her usual prickly words? Was she going to laugh and tell me she'd been pranking me the whole time and that she still hated my guts? I didn't know what to expect from her anymore. Which was very unsettling. I kind of preferred the old, predictable Butt Breath who was routinely and consistently mean. She was the devil I knew. This new devil, who was smiley and friendly and 'nice', was totally doing my head in!

After a long, painful pause, she just shrugged and walked off. 'Suit yourself.' I finally exhaled, glad to have dodged another verbal beating.

Phew.

Back to exams. Most kids hate them. Truth is, up until this year, I did too. I hated having to study.

The pressure. Will I pass? Will I fail? Will my parents be mad or proud? Then there's the anticipation – waiting for the exam day to arrive. In short, there's not much to like about exam week. Except for some reason, this year, I was loving it sideways. Living and breathing it like it was Christmas, Naw-Rúz and Hanukkah all at the same time.

I think it's because it gave me purpose. A short-term goal that I knew I'd be around to see the result of. And I was actually enjoying the study aspect of it. Finding comfort in throwing myself into the books.

Somehow I felt cocooned. Warm and safe. I felt like whatever I was learning, all that knowledge, was coming with me when I died. My body might wither and conk out and eventually get eaten by worms but my expanding mind would transcend all that. It was forever mine. I felt sure about that. Sure that there are only two things in this world that are indestructible. Two things that can never be nuked or annihilated.

LOVE
and
KNOWLEDGE.

So I was working hard to acquire all the knowledge I could. I wanted to cram it in until it came pouring out of my ears.

I threw myself into every subject. History, Geography, Art, Science and even Maths. But my favourite without a doubt was English. When words are woven together like a tapestry and someone breathes their soul into it, the result is other-worldly. Sounds pretentious but it's true.

My exam assignment for English was to write a story. A pretty simple task. Everyone in the class moaned and complained about it for weeks but I saw it as my chance to shine. Not only would I write a story – I would write THE story. Of the last year of my life on Earth.

Ding!

Did the penny just drop?

Yes, you are reading my English assignment. It was meant to be a few pages but it kind of got out of hand. Oops! It's looking more like my debut novel.

Mr Evans better give me an 'A' for this or I'll haunt his house!

Jokes aside, writing this has made me realise what a gift life is. You may have been wondering about the title – let me explain ...

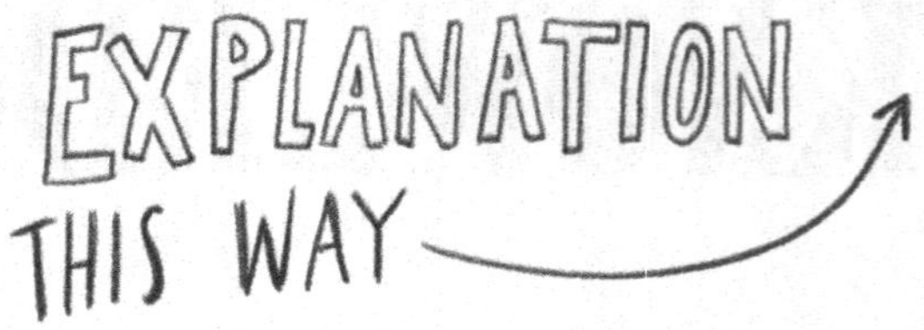

Exit through the gift shop

Have you ever been to the zoo? Or a museum? Or any kind of amusement park? If the answer is yes, then you'll know what I'm talking about. The only way out is through the gift shop. Whether you like it or not!

Your parents hate it 'cause they have to cough up more money for all the things that you didn't know you wanted or needed!

You can go through life blindly, not even realising how much better things would be with your very own elephant mug. Am I right or am I right?

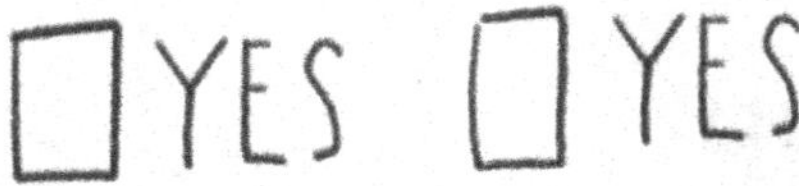

If you haven't twigged yet, this is another one of my brilliant metaphors. Although I genuinely love all the random trinkets you find in gift shops, the reason I chose it as a title for my book is that life kind of works in the same way. When you're on your way out, you are forced to look at gifts you would ordinarily bypass. Not helium balloons or magnetic sand. Different kinds of gifts.

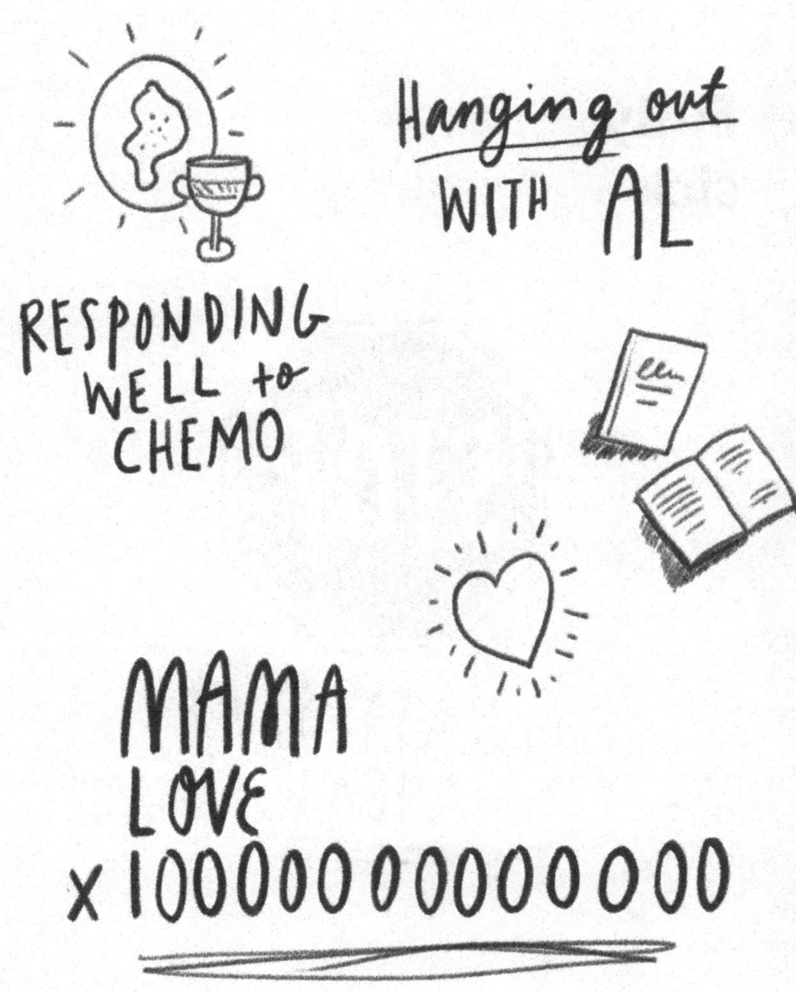

There are endless gifts to appreciate on the way out of this 'Life' gig. But before I get too carried away and glorify death too much, let's just take a minute to breathe and remember that dying . . . like living, has its ups and downs.

Fully sick

Feel free to skip this chapter if you're one of those people who gets queasy and uncomfortable when it comes to hearing about the details of sickness. Don't worry, I won't even know you're skipping and even if I did, there's no way I'd be judgey. Before I got cancer, I couldn't even cope when Destiny (my stepsister – bet you'd totally forgotten about her!) got chicken pox. The fever, the floppiness, the gooey then scabby spots! I just couldn't handle it so I stayed at Mum's until she got better. And not just 'cause it's catchy but because I didn't like being around disease. So, basically, what I'm trying to say is that if you're like me, I'll meet you at the next chapter.

Just waiting for you all to leave.

For those of you still here, here's what happens when you get chemo. There are actually so many different side effects but thankfully I didn't get all of them. Here are a few that I *did* get.

Nausea – feels like I'm on a cruise ship trying to steady myself. Or like there's an alien in my stomach trying to break out. Usually gets better if I lie down. Which isn't always possible. Especially when I'm at school.

Vomiting – doesn't happen too much but when it does, there's no waiting until I find a suitable place to puke. It's BLUUUURRRGGGH all over the place. Very embarrassing. Especially the time I did it all over the self-service cash register at Woolies. It got all over Wanda's left hand (she was scanning some gum for me at the time) and my brand-new suede shoes.

side note: vom + suede = very bad combo

Hair loss – okay, so this is the hardest one to deal with. Nothing can really prepare you for it. Clumps falling out in the shower, on your pillow, wherever you go.

Like a shedding puppy.

Or autumn leaves. Falling ...

and falling ...

and falling.

falling

falling falling

falling falling

Until you're left with a patchy pattern, which makes your head look like a slightly out-of-focus globe of the world.

It's a terrifying feeling. No matter how much the doctors try to prepare you, it's still a shock. The first time I got a handful of hair, I was casually throwing my hair up into a ponytail like I've done a million times before. Mum was driving me to school. I think I actually screamed. She slammed on the brakes and I burst into tears. It was horrible. And I'm not gonna lie – it hasn't really improved over time. It's still super depressing.

All the positive mantras in the world (and believe me, my mum knows them all and recites each one to me daily!) don't help. Lately she's taken to putting these cringey one-liners on post-it notes and sticking them up around the house.

BLUUUURRRGGH!

Who writes this stuff?! Makes me want to vom all over again.

How do I tell Mum that her 'uplifting' quotes are actually making me feel worse? I have screwed up and binned every single cheesy post-it note she's put up but she's not getting the message.

The thing is that when you're losing your hair, no shift in focus, whether it be diving head-first into maths homework and tackling a curly algebra equation or playing Jedi mind tricks on Spanx by hiding his kitty litter, will make you feel better about yourself.

There's no use trying to find the butterfly in this trash heap. The horrible fact of the matter is that you're not even 13 yet and you're bald. Suddenly the cancer is visible. And it's staring back at you in the mirror. That's when the *really* dark thoughts come. And sometimes, despite your best attempts to make them disappear, they hit you like a freight train.

I'm bald. I'm ugly. No boy will ever like me now. No boy will ever like me anyway, because why would anyone bother liking a dying girl?

But before I go too far down the dark hole of all the terrible ways a pre-teen girl can feel when she's going through chemo, I'll tell you this. Sometimes when you're deep, DEEP down in a ditch (yah, metaphor again) and it's so dark that you can't even see your own hand in front of you, sometimes, just sometimes, there's an AI who comes along and shines a light and helps pull you out of the well.

Wiggin' out – Al's finest moment

'Ana, Al's . . . um, Al is . . . here to see you.'

There was something in my mum's voice when she called out to me from the front door that made me think this wasn't an ordinary visit from Al. I was lying on the couch, feeling sorry for myself. Also feeling sick. Again, feeling sorry + feeling sick = deadly combo (pardon the pun, poor taste, I know).

'Tell him I'm too sick for visitors,' I said, barely able to muster up the strength to even speak. But Al wasn't going to be turned away. Not today. He pushed the door wide open and presented himself in the middle of my lounge room in all his magnificent glory.

'How do I look?'

He struck a goofy pose.

'I've got a good side . . .'

He turned to one side, then confidently swung to the other.

'. . . and a spectacular side!'

I burst out laughing.

He was wearing the BIGGEST, brightest, most outrageous wig you've ever seen. Imagine Elvis's hair – on steroids. I'd call it a fro but it was beyond a fro. It was the mother of all fros. And it was orange. A kind of deep, burnt, glittery orange that hurt your eyes.

Teased at the front so it formed a massive bouffant, then it tapered in at the sides like a mullet and formed a kind of rat's tail at the back.

It was SO bad that it was good. Brilliant, in fact.

I sat up and admired this work of art. Speechless. Al did a few more spins so that I could get a good look from every angle.

'What on earth?'

He looked at me deadpan. 'Don't hate me because I'm beautiful!'

'You. Look. Ridiculous!' I said.

Al then produced a big black garbage bag, reached in and pulled out another wig. This one was spiky and short and gold!

'What do you think of this one?' he asked.

'Also ridic!'

I couldn't stop laughing as he whipped off the first wig and put on the second.

'Oh, that's much more your style,' said my mum from the doorway. Al then went on to try on one crazy wig after another. Turned out he'd spent his entire savings plus some money that he borrowed from his parents to buy this incredible collection of outrageous wigs from eBay. He said that the only way to navigate my way through this hair-loss nightmare (my words, not his) was by embracing it. And celebrating. And laughing. And being totally and utterly ridiculous.

'A bald head calls for a bold wig. Get it? Bald – bold? It's a play on words. Kind of a dad joke. But a good one, don't you reckon? So, do you love it or do you love it?'

I was so touched by this mighty act of love.

But there was no way I could wear any of those wigs out in public. I didn't know how to break it to him. So I ummm-ed ... and I ahhh-ed ... then ummm-ed ... and ahhh-ed again.

As I was thinking about how to let him down gently, he yanked me off the couch and said, 'If you're thinking about how to let me down gently, stop. You can't. I'm not taking no for an answer.'

GULP.

I was going to have to tackle this a different way. My mind was racing. How was I going to squirm my way out of this?

Al, who I swear can read my mind, turned it up a notch and launched into a monologue about how he was going to wear a different outrageous wig to school each day from now until my hair grew back and if I were any kind of a friend, I wouldn't let him wear a crazy wig on his own. He said that he'd bought 14 wigs for the both of us and if we rotated then switched, we could rock a different look every single day on a fortnightly cycle.

He'd done the maths.

He was all over it.

And ultimately his argument was this: if people were gonna stare and judge and whisper because you were losing your hair, then the best way to combat that was to triple your dose of confidence (even if you were faking it) and REALLY give 'em something to talk about. Once again I was left speechless. I couldn't argue with Al's logic. Nor could I let him show up to school looking like a nutter wearing these wigs by himself.

'We're in this together, Ana. So what d'ya say?'

I could barely hold back the tears. Not sad tears. Happy tears. Tears that come when you can't believe how lucky you are to score a bestie like Al. So I said yes. And I somehow managed not to cry. That's more than could be said for Mum who leapt towards Al and hugged him, tears streaming down her face. She didn't say a word but gave him a look that said 'thank you from the bottom of my heart', then left the room. Al and I tried on the wigs and laughed. For the first time ever I took selfies and uploaded them onto my Insta.

Me! Selfies!

Never thought I'd see the day, but this was an exception. Here are a few examples:

#MERMAIDHAIR

#theColour purple

#BIG HAIR DON'T CARE

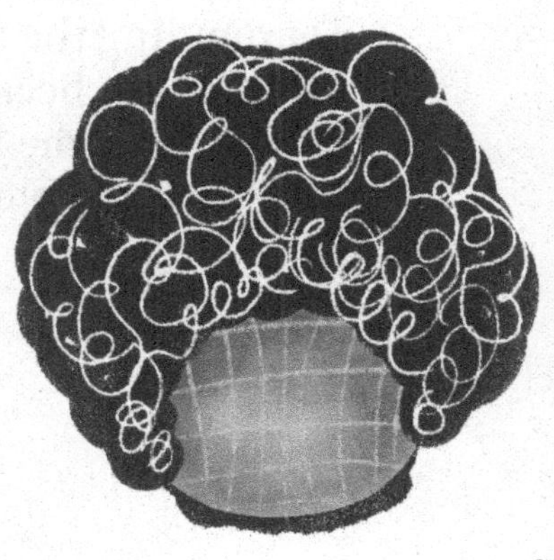

#HAIR GOALS

School corridor catwalk

It was all my idea. Not only was I going to wear these crazy wigs to school, I was going to strut doing it. Honestly, I do not know what came over me. I don't know if it was the wigs or the whole 'leaving planet Earth' thing that gave me the confidence but suddenly, and out of nowhere, I had chutzpah.

Chutzpah (*hoot*-spa)
Noun, origin Hebrew
Extreme self-confidence or audacity. Not in an arrogant, up-yourself kind of way but in a Beyoncé-killing-it-at-Coachella kind of way. Demanding the attention of those around you, because you know that you've got some kind of magic that will bring people joy.

The first day we did the catwalk, I didn't know what to expect. Al made a grand entrance. Asked everyone to back up to their lockers and clear the corridor. Then he pumped the music. Yep, you guessed it – Beyoncé. Blasted it out from his portable speaker. No one knew what was happening ... until I entered.

Rocking a purple punk mohawk, I strutted my way past the Science block as if I were showcasing the latest Gucci range on a Paris catwalk during Fashion Week. Al then put on his wig and joined me on the catwalk. We did a super hammy, over-the-top catwalk strut together and here's what happened next.

Everyone lost their minds.

They started cheering and dancing and clapping. Teachers came rushing out of their classrooms to see what was going on. The atmosphere was euphoric. If it was possible to measure love on a mass scale, in those few minutes, it would have been bursting off the charts.

Even though no one had said a single word to me about my cancer up to that point, they were saying it now. With their cheers. They were saying:

WE SEE YOU.

YOU GOT THIS.

I'M SORRY.

YOU ARE NOT ALONE.

And before I knew it, the catwalk strut had turned into an impromptu dance party and everyone was dancing along with me and Al. This is the kind of thing that would normally have the teachers shouting and giving out detentions. But not today. Today they were smiling. And dancing. Mr Sahabdeen was wiping away tears. The big softie.

For those three minutes and 55 seconds (that was the length of the song), time stood still. And I realised that love doesn't always come in packages that you'd expect. Sometimes, people don't know how to cope with grief. And sometimes that grief manifests as joy. The joy we were all feeling in that corridor would not have been possible without the pain of me dying. Weird, huh?

One thing I've learnt on this cancer journey is that sometimes life comes at you all at once. The good, the bad and the ugly. And the only thing to do is to swallow it whole. The joy and the pain. The yin and the yang. The light and the dark. They're inseparable and beautiful at the same time.

So the school corridor catwalk became a sporadic ritual. Is that even a thing? Sporadic, by definition, is the opposite of ritual. But this is a ritual that happens sporadically. Every now and then, before the morning bell, without any formal discussion or planning, everyone gathers to wait for Al and me to arrive. We don't know when they'll be lining the corridors, waiting for a dance party, but we're always prepared.

And boy, do we arrive in style!

Each time with a different wig and a different song. And we always deliver. These 'catwalks' have broken down all the barriers. I'm now getting hugs, high fives and a lot of buzz about all my different wigs. You could say Al and I have become school celebs. And we're enjoying every moment of the ride.

#meandthedyinggirl

Boom!

I guess it was time for Alyssa to rear her (pretty) ugly head again. She'd been so quiet for so long, I'd almost forgotten about her. Between the chemo and the catwalks and exam week, I hadn't stopped to think about her for ages. I mean, she was still stalking me and taking selfies but for some reason I'd grown accustomed to it. Or maybe I just didn't care. Either way, every time she'd sidle up and snap a pic I somehow managed to endure it. Sometimes I'd even smile. And with everything else that was going on, I stopped thinking about why. I stopped questioning her motive. I just stopped thinking about her altogether now that she wasn't hurling abuse at me daily. She was out of my life. Maybe that's why I'd been feeling all euphoric about dying and talking about 'gifts' like I was on some kind of happy gas.

It was Al who brought it to my attention. One simple hashtag on Instagram.

#meandthedyinggirl

He wanted me to hear it from him and not stumble upon it myself (like he had) on Insta.

Next-level evil

Every single photo that Alyssa had taken had been uploaded onto her new account, which was dedicated entirely to me and my imminent death.

Yes, you read that correctly. Butt Breath was no longer just another schoolyard bully. She wasn't the clichéd mean girl you see in films or hear about from your friends. She was sick. Like, really sick. Sick in the head. And somehow she'd attracted all the sickos on the internet because this account had actual followers. Not millions, but enough.

While my family and my school community surrounded me with love and filled my days with laughter and joy, Alyssa and her band of horrible trolls were delighting in watching me slowly deteriorate.

I'm just going to give you a moment to digest this. I needed it too.

It took me a long time to wrap my head around what Al was telling me. Truth is, my brain checked out again. I went on one of my brain breaks while he gently tried to help me understand what was going on. It felt like my head was spinning at a billion kilometres an hour and rocketing towards the sun.

This one was a particularly tricky brain break to come back from. But eventually I did. There was no escaping this reality. Just as I was writing about the last year of my life in this book, Alyssa was doing the same, but with a dark twist. A countdown. In some pics, she was doing a 'thinking pose', with a ticking clock Insta sticker whacked on the side. Other pics had quiz questions. Who could guess what disease I had? You could choose from a range of deadly cancers. I couldn't believe it. This monster was interactive. Butt Breath was getting so much attention from these death-obsessed emo types and she was loving it.

Why was she doing this? Maybe she thought it was a bad look (even for her) to keep bullying 'the dying girl' out in the open, so she had to go underground. Find another way to get attention. Maybe she actually had some mental disorder?

Or maybe she was just next-level evil.

SEE GRAPH

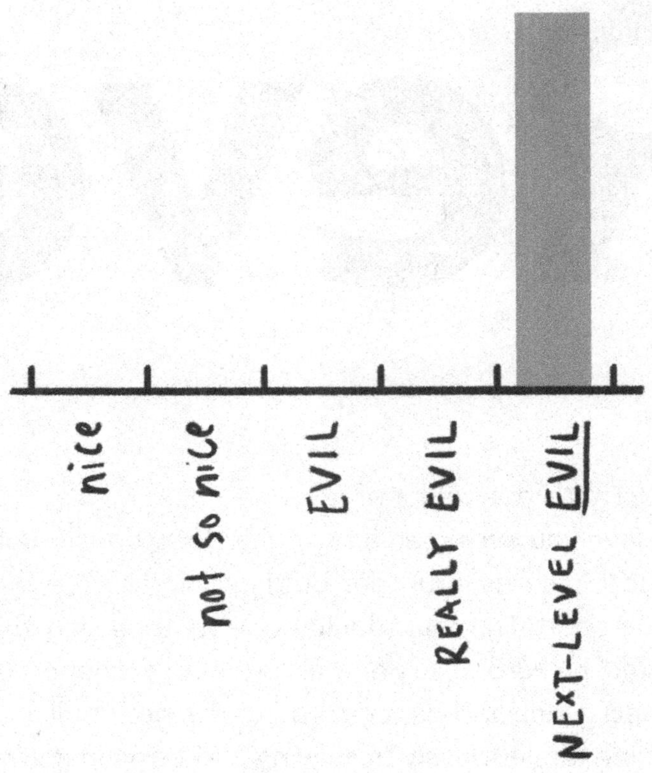

Whatever her reason, enough was enough. She had crossed a line and by crossing that line, something in me had snapped. I was mad. Mad as hell. And I wasn't going to take this one lying down. This time I was going to fight back. This time I wanted . . .

Reve

RED. That's the colour of revenge.

Have you ever seen a bullfight? They consider it a sport in some countries but I just find it cruel. A blood sport. The matador (a dude wearing skin-tight, blingy knickerbockers and a matching, too-short jacket) glides and dances around the poor bull, teasing it relentlessly by waving a RED rag in its face.

That in itself doesn't seem so bad, except here's the problem.

The bull clearly has 'RED' issues. It's a triggering colour for him. So when he sees the big, velvety RED rag waved in his face, he loses it. Goes totally ballistic and charges towards it. The matador lives for this reaction. Tormenting the bull is what he does best. That's his gig. So he turns it up a notch with his RED rag flamenco tease, eventually turning the bull into a full-blown rage monster. That tsunami of RED-hot

nge!

fury flooding the bull's brain when he's being taunted was exactly what I felt too.

I was seeing RED.

I wanted revenge. Sweet, sweet revenge. And I was going to get it.

But where do you even start? I had no experience in this kind of thing. Wanting to gouge someone's eyes out is one thing. Doing it is another.

Al encouraged me to ignore it. Not to let it get to me. I agreed – mostly to shut him up. But I didn't want common sense or the 'greater good' to get in the way this time. I'd always done the right thing and for what? It had got me nowhere. In all the years that Alyssa had bullied me, I had never once dobbed, retaliated or even confronted her. So, this time, without thinking it through, in my clumsy, unsophisticated way, I decided to confront her.

Face-off

A few days passed. Somehow I remained strong and resisted the urge to look up the nasty comments online. But as time went on, I grew more furious. Which is why, when I saw Butt Breath before first period, at approximately 8.47 am on Wednesday morning, walking with two of her cronies towards the Science block, I was ready. With my heart pounding at a hundred miles per hour, I made my approach.

She was kind of shocked to see me walking towards her with purpose. I think she could tell something was different in me. Something had changed.

'Hi, Ana, are you okay? I mean, I know you're not *okay*, but are you okay right now?' She sniggered at her sidekicks.

They sniggered back – in unison. Her back-up buddies did everything together. They travelled as a pack. Like wolves. They strutted together, ate lunch together, took all the same classes and failed them together. If you squinted long enough, they'd actually blend into each other. You couldn't see where one ended and the next one began. They were an eye-rolling, hair-flicking, mega-mean posse all rolled into one. And I needed them gone. I took a deep breath and made my demand. 'I need to talk to you. Alone!'

Alyssa seemed amused by my stern request but she dismissed her friends immediately. 'It's okay, I got this.'

They pranced off, their stupid ponytails swinging from side to side. Alyssa waved them goodbye then turned to face me. She was looking down on me. Either she had grown ten inches since I saw her last, or I had shrunk, because she seemed to tower above me. Her glistening, golden hair blowing ever so gently in the breeze, like one of those cheesy shampoo commercials. I turned back to see if she'd brought her own wind machine.

Nope. She was just annoyingly glamorous. And the world was her studio.

She stood there, looking at me. Hand on hip. Waiting.

'Problem?'

I tried to gather my thoughts. Why was the world spinning extra fast today? Focus, Ana. Focus!

Alyssa rolled her eyes, as if I was a monumental waste of time.

'Helloooooo? Earth to Ana. What do you want to talk to me about?'

I dug deep for whatever dregs of courage I had in the pit of my belly and finally spoke.

'Me and the dying girl? Really?'

She smiled. A knowing, triumphant smile.

'I was wondering how long it'd take you to catch on.'

'How could you?' I said, my voice breaking.

Then her tone switched from condescending to vicious.

'Oh boo-freaking-hoo. You may think that the world revolves around you just because you're dying, but newsflash – nobody actually cares!'

I couldn't breathe.

'Nobody gives a flying fart. Except for the fans I've found online. They're really into you dying.' She laughed. I couldn't believe what was happening. My ears started to burn. They felt like they were on fire. And the pounding of my heart was so loud, I was sure she could hear it.

'Did you think that I was suddenly going to love your guts because you're kicking the bucket? You have no idea how much mileage I'm getting out of your march towards the finish line. I reckon I've started a whole new movement of death-lovin' zombies online.'

She then put her hand on my shoulder. 'So, thank you. Feels odd to say thank you for dying but it's been really good for me ... anyway, I've got Maths. One more selfie before I go?'

She pulled out her phone and flipped it around to take a selfie. And that's when it happened.

I PUNCHED HER.
HARD.
IN THE FACE.

I don't even remember doing it. Nor did I decide to do it. It's like I was suddenly possessed. I clobbered her so hard that she hit the ground. She screamed.

'My nose! You've broken my nose!'

My world crashed in on itself. I felt like I was having an out-of-body experience. Just watching what was unfolding from above. With no sense of self or connection to the person who had just thrown that punch. Who was I even?

I felt sick. Did I really just do that? I had never, ever punched anyone before in my life. Thugs threw punches. Not me. Alyssa seemed just as shocked as I was.

'You're gonna pay for this, you stupid cow!'

As I was trying to process this alternate reality, where I, sweet reasonable Ana, had just committed grievous bodily harm, I noticed that Alyssa's phone was still in her hand. She was filming the whole thing. Filming herself screaming and wiping blood from her face. Filming me, standing there, looking petrified. A crowd gathered very quickly. It all must've happened in a matter of a few seconds but it felt like centuries. Like I was traipsing through mud in slow motion.

Alyssa Anderson was on the ground. She was screaming and bleeding. And it was because of me. I did that.

I felt guilty. Confused. Terrified. This wasn't the revenge I was thinking of. This wasn't revenge at all. This was going to land me in enormous trouble. And the worst part about it? Alyssa was loving it. She was going to have more content for her stupid page. More attention for herself. She had lured me to a trap and I had fallen straight in. I'd taken the bait like an absolute amateur. I tried to wrap my head around what had just happened. I felt both numb and on fire at the same time. Where was Al when I needed him most? My eyes darted around the yard. I couldn't see him. All I saw were stunned faces and people rushing to Alyssa's aid. And so I ran.

I ran as fast and as far as I possibly could. I may have run all the way home. I may have run to Slovakia. I don't actually remember. Everything became a blur. The next thing I knew I was sitting at the kitchen table at Mum's house stirring sugar into my tea. Dad was there too. And Plastic Pat.

What happened? Was a War Council called? I remember wishing the earth would open up and swallow me. But no such luck. Here we were. Having tea. Persian tea.

Tea break

WE INTERRUPT THIS
VERY IMPORTANT **EMERGENCY SITUATION TO DISCUSS ANOTHER VERY IMPORTANT MATTER.**

Persian tea.

Persian tea deserves its own chapter. And I want it on the record that it is superior to all other kinds of teas. Yes, all of them. No offence to the English, I know they take their tea very seriously. But don't talk to me about Earl *this* or Irish *that*, Darjeeling or chamomile. Persian tea beats them all. Hands down. It has an aroma that puts you immediately at ease. It's more than just tea. It's like some sort of magic potion that makes the world right again. It cures all ills (except maybe cancer).

That perfect combination of black tea, cardamom and rosewater resets the balance of the universe when equilibrium has been lost. Don't ask me how. It just does. Most people don't give caffeinated drinks to their children, but in my family we always have a pot brewing because you never know what life is going to throw at you. And in this case, it's thrown a punch. Literally!

The aftermath

I stirred some nabát (rock sugar) into my tea. I was mesmerised by the way the tea swirled around and around in my cup . . . I imagined myself shrinking to the size of a fairyfly (that's the smallest insect in the world) and surfing atop the nabát, in a sea of sweet, warm Persian tea.
Ah, how wondrous
that would be.

'You can't just go around punching people in the face, Anahita!' Mum's words seemed to circle the room. I kept stirring my tea as she went on and on about the perils of 'resorting to violence', as if I were some psycho assassin who was leaving a trail of blood and a hideous body count behind me.

Thank God for Dad. He wasn't having any of it.

'She doesn't "go around" punching people. She's never laid a finger on an ant, let alone a person. Let's not lose perspective here!'

He wasn't taking a moral position or trying to school me on right and wrong. He was on my side before he heard any of the facts. Faithfully and unequivocally on my side. As far as he was concerned, there *was* no 'other side'. If I had whacked someone in the face, knocked them to the ground and made them bleed, then they had it comin', and it was *them* who we should be questioning.

Honestly, I could not love my dad more if I tried.

'But what happened, Ana joon? It's so unlike you to do something like this.' If Mum was calling me 'joon' she couldn't have been *too* angry with me. But she still wanted answers. She was struggling to understand. 'You've never had issues with anyone at school before.'

She had no idea. And I had no energy to explain. Besides, my tea was getting cold. Dad chimed in and tried to break things down for her. He talked about how nothing is as it was before. That dealing with cancer is life-changing. And stressful. And if kids were picking on me because of my illness, or my hair loss, or whatever ... then it was understandable that I would lose control. Not right, but understandable. Mum wasn't satisfied with this justification but she could see how sad I was, so she let it go. It broke my heart to see her so disappointed in me. I wanted to tell her that I was disappointed in me too. That even though Alyssa was a poisonous snake, I hated the fact that she had turned me into a rage monster. A bull triggered by the RED rag. She had unleashed my inner 'gangsta' and I wasn't happy about it. It didn't gel with the image I had of myself. I wanted to tell Mum that I was just as shocked as she was by this incident.

But I didn't say anything.
I just drank my tea.
And Mum drank hers.
And eventually everyone calmed down.

(Told you Persian tea cures all ills!)

Suspension

Ms Longbottom suspended me for three days. I guess she had to. School policy, **blah, blah, blah**. She told me that she was 'disappointed' in me and that I should spend this time thinking about my actions. But I reckon there was a twinkle in her eye. Maybe I was imagining it, but it felt like she was reciting lines from the 'School Principal' script when actually, deep down inside, she was glad that someone had finally given Alyssa a knuckle sandwich. Either that or she was going easy on me because, you know, I'm dying. Dying does have its perks. Like a get-out-of-jail-free card. Not that I got off scot-free. But it could've been worse. I could've been expelled.

I spent my suspension days at Dad and Wanda's. Mainly helping Wanda. And hanging out with my step-sibs – playing hide and seek and watching a lot of Cartoon Network. Al would message me almost hourly. Like a Hollywood reporter, he spared no detail about the buzz back at school. He was totally in his element. All he needed was a mic and a TV crew.

Omigosh, Ana, you're not gonna believe this. She just walked into History and sat DIRECTLY opposite me. Why would she do that? Whyyyy? Getting a death stare as I type. Lol

He texted like he spoke. Too much and too fast.

How's her nose?

Swollen. Bit blue. Still can't believe you punched her #madrespect

He told me that the Ana/Alyssa showdown was all anybody could talk about. The story had been told and retold and exaggerated a hundred, thousand, million, billion, gazillion times.

See what I did there?

Schoolyard gossip had turned that one punch into a brawl. A full-blown rumble in the jungle. To be honest, I wasn't surprised. Kids love drama. I told Al not to believe the fake news. He laughed and made me promise that I'd tell him all the gory details when I saw him. I dutifully crossed my heart.

When can I see you btw?

I'm suspended. Officially under house arrest.

I'll come over after school. We can talk through a glass partition, on those old phones, like in the movies. When crims get visitors from the outside.

I actually LOL-ed.

Later, Al.

I expect you to be wearing an orange jumpsuit!

I tossed the phone aside and sank into the couch. Spanx pranced by and threw me a testy, exasperated look that clearly said, 'Pfft, humans and their petty affairs!'

I sat for ages. Staring up at the cracks in the ceiling. I should've been thinking about my terrible actions but my mind kept creeping back to the next part of my revenge plot. My plans had been derailed because I'd lost control, but I wasn't done yet. You see, the thing about being bullied is that it messes with your psyche. It beats you down and makes you kinda crazy. I'd taken so much trash talk, put-downs and trolling from Butt Breath over the years, but this last kick, the hashtag, was unforgivable. They say that revenge is a dish best served cold. I'm not exactly sure what that means but what I do know is that the punch was just the entrée. Ordered off the wrong menu. A distraction. I couldn't call it quits now. I had to sort out my thoughts and come up with something good. A proper revenge plan. My mind started going down some pretty dark paths. And before you start guessing, let me tell you that violence was out of the question. Inflicting bodily harm is not my jam. I'm a pacifist by nature. Besides, I'd already done that, so . . . ☑

No, I wanted to hurt her the way she'd been hurting me all these years. I wanted her to know what it feels like to be humiliated, scared and low. I wanted her to experience the same pain in the same way. But being a loudmouth ruthless bully isn't my jam either. I was facing a conundrum. Plotting and executing revenge was hard work. The Devil's work. And I wasn't fully equipped.

So I decided to enlist help from someone even less qualified than me.

Al.

Al – the 'ideas man'

There are two theories about what constitutes a 'true friend'. One is that a true friend will act as a mirror. Reflecting your good and bad qualities and always helping you to be your best self. When they see you taking the wrong fork in the road, they stop you and knock some sense into you before showing you the right path.

The other theory is that a true friend will ride with you no matter what. If you're speeding along the highway at 150 kilometres per hour in the wrong direction towards oncoming traffic, they shout 'LET'S GOOO!' and jump in the passenger seat, risking their own life in the name of solidarity.

Al is the latter. He's my Ride or Die.

After making me re-enact every moment of 'the punch' and laughing till he almost turned blue, he pulled out a pencil, paper and a clipboard. He made it clear that plotting revenge is serious business. We needed to have regular meetings, take minutes, delegate duties and execute with precision.

This wasn't going to be another clumsy schoolyard punch. This was going to be beautiful. I have to be honest . . . this side of Al, while very amusing, scared me a little. I never knew he had a dark side. But I guess everyone does. Ahem, me included!

We brainstormed and made a list of Ultimate Revenge ideas. No idea was too dumb or too evil. We told Wanda we were 'studying' so she brought us tea, cheese toasties and chocolate. It was brilliant. This was the beginning of a revolution and it couldn't be done on empty bellies. I'm pretty sure that Wanda would've approved of our cunning scheming and brought us even more snacks for fuel but I didn't want to make her an accomplice. She has enough to worry about without getting caught up in my mess.

So, we laughed and ate and laughed some more. Al madly jotted notes onto his clipboard.

It was therapeutic and much more fun than I had imagined. No wonder good people are drawn to the dark side. Anakin Skywalker/Darth Vader: case in point. The line between good and evil is a thin one. I felt myself slipping over to the dark side. And I'll be honest, it felt good. Just *talking* about getting revenge on Alyssa made me feel powerful. No longer a victim. And to my surprise I didn't feel any guilt. Not even a twinge. I felt completely justified. Almost like a superhero who was finally going to get the bad guy and free the people of the city from a life of terror and suffering. Every now and then Al would pause and ask me if we were doing the right thing.

'Um, are you really sure you wanna do this?'

'Don't chicken out on me now, Al.'

'No, no . . . definitely not chickening out. Only chickens chicken out. And I'm no chicken.'

'Stop saying chicken.'

'I was just wondering if *you* were having second thoughts. If you wanted to . . . maybe . . . abort the mission?'

'WHAT?!'

No way. I wasn't having it. Why should we do 'the right thing' while Alyssa continued with her witchcraft? She had uploaded the 'punch' video before the blood had even dried on her nose! And she was loving the attention. The 'likes'. The sympathetic comments from strangers who hadn't seen the years and years of bullying that had culminated in that punch. So no, I told Al there was no way we were aborting the mission. For the first time since that fateful day in Year 5 when Alyssa first clapped eyes on me and made me her target, I felt fearless. I had nothing to lose and everything to gain. We were going to get her back and it was going to be beautiful. Al apologised for his momentary lapse in judgement and we resumed work. After many hours of plotting we came up with a shortlist of ideas:

Ultimate Revenge List

1. Raid her drawer and rub itching powder on all her undies (this involves breaking and entering so perhaps not practical).
2. Steal her phone and change all her contact names to characters from *Frozen*.
3. Take her hand sanitiser and replace the contents with superglue.
4. Write a book about my life with her as the villain who finally gets her comeuppance.
5. Put laxatives in her drink bottle.
6. Hide sardines in the back of her locker.
7. Sneak into her house during the night (which obviously requires the 'breaking and entering' thing again) and cut off her golden locks. Give her a bowl cut. She's so vain, she'd never recover.
8. Call Luigi's Pizzeria and order 50 shrimp, broccoli and anchovy pizzas, with extra soy cheese, to her home address.

BRAINSTORM:
Drink bottle
GLUE
EVIL vs. GENIUS
CHOP CHOP
STINKY
FROZEN
ITCHING POWDER
TROUBLE
Chicken Chicken
Chicken Chicken
Chicken Chicken
REVENGE!

The list went on but somehow all these ideas left me unsatisfied. They were more like childish pranks than revenge. If I really wanted to hurt her, I'd have to go to the next level. Play the game by her rules. Put my conscience aside and think of the one thing that would damage her the most. Something that would stain her reputation. That would follow her for the rest of her life.

And then it came to me.

Entrapment
Noun
The act of tricking someone into doing something illegal so that you can prosecute them for it. Not forcing them . . . just enticing them. Like dangling a metaphorical carrot in front of their piercing blue eyes. Here, little bunny, do what you always do . . . come and devour this juicy, delicious carrot! No strings attached. Promise. And then – *SNAP!* Gotcha! You've been punk'd. Trapped. Entrapped!

You see, I didn't really have to do anything to Alyssa. I'd just have to expose her for the monster she truly is. Expose her, not only to her friends and family and community, but to the law. I figured that there must be laws against what she's done to me. So, Al and I went from plotting silly pranks to researching online harassment laws. There are volumes of laws and by-laws and a lot of grey areas when it comes to cyberbullies. But ultimately it all comes down to this:

> Under the ***Criminal Code Act 1995*** it is an offence to use the internet, social media or a telephone to menace, harass or cause offence. The maximum penalty for this offence is three years' imprisonment or a fine of more than $30,000.

Facts.

Who knew? The law also states that 'stalking' is an offence. Now, you may think Alyssa isn't a stalker, but the truth is that she has been stalking and harassing me for years.

According to the same Act:

> Stalking involves a persistent course of conduct by a person against a victim, which intends to make them feel fearful, uncomfortable, offended or harassed.

Al and I looked at each other. This was it. This was the way to take her out. Dragged by her tail all the way to juvie. This was the perfect revenge. Actually, it would be better than revenge. It would be justice. And it suited me much more. Ana, the Avenging Angel, not the Puncher of Bullies.

That image never sat right with me. I know Al was a big fan but it made me feel all wonky and out of balance. A little bit seasick.

This way, Butt Breath would have a criminal record. Even if that record got wiped when she turned 18 (which apparently it does), her reputation would be mud. This would follow her for her whole life. All these years of abuse would be her ultimate undoing. A life sentence that she had given to herself unknowingly. Because that's how karma works.

Karma (*kaa-muh*)
Noun, origin Sanskrit
The spiritual principle of cause and effect. When you do good, good things happen to you, and when you do bad, bad things happen to you. What goes around comes around. Like a boomerang. Like that time Plastic Pat left his puppy in the car while he got some 'work done', and the pup did a big fat number two and got stinky, brown doo-doo wedged into every crease and corner of Pat's swanky new upholstery – that was karma.

There was a certain pleasure in knowing that I didn't have to get my hands dirty in order for there to be justice. I just had to shine a light on Butt Breath's dark and sinister soul. And that, I was more than happy to do.

Ana & Al (*CSI*)

It was going to take some work to gather all the evidence we needed to take to the police. The first thing we did was to take a screenshot of every page and every horrible comment on her account. That meant reading through them all and some of it was very hard to take. People I didn't even know were placing bets on when I would die. Actual bets. Butt Breath had unleashed the powers of darkness. Al decided halfway through the evidence-gathering process that he should take charge so that I wasn't exposed to any more nastiness. And I let him. Even though we had a game plan, every comment was a blow. A punch to the head. Much harder and more painful than the one I had delivered to Alyssa in the schoolyard.

It got me thinking about these faceless people hiding behind their keyboards. Why did these trolls troll? Who were they, even? Creepy middle-aged losers who live in their mums' basements? Or regular, respectable folk with day jobs? Or kids? Kids like Alyssa Anderson, who look pretty, walk pretty and talk pretty when everyone is watching but who have ugly insides? All I knew was that there were lots of them. Not just one or two. These miserable, hate-spewing keyboard warriors were out there, feeding off each other and fighting over the scraps, like vultures. I was relieved to close the tab on their ugly world. And thankful to Al for doing the grunt work.

After collecting the online evidence, it was time for some video proof. Getting Butt Breath to dig her own grave was easier than we thought. All we had to do was to ever so gently poke the bear.

Poking the bear
Colloquial expression
Doing something that may provoke a negative response from someone. Obviously poking a bear is not a smart move. That beast ain't gonna like it. At best, she'll growl in your face to express her anger and at worst, she'll hunt you down and eat you. She'll start by biting off your head and swallowing it whole, then she'll chow down on your limbs one by one and finish up by using your hair to floss her teeth. My top tip for the day: do not, I repeat, do NOT poke bears. Especially ones with flowing blonde hair and perfect teeth.

Of course, I never take my own advice. So here I am, knee-deep in the biggest bear-poking act of all time.

Phase 1 – Entrapment

The most elaborate trap we set was what Al likes to refer to as 'The Secret Diary of Ana the Mole'. A twist on his all-time favourite book, *The Secret Diary of Adrian Mole*. And he assured me that my title of 'mole' wasn't a reference to my character. Rather, it indicated my role as an undercover spy slash justice warrior.

Here's what we did. I wrote a pretend diary. In this pretend diary, I pretended that I had a crush on a pretend boy, who we called Tennyson. A name weird enough that it didn't seem made up. In this pretend universe, Ana is about to meet Tennyson face to face for the first time. Up till now, they've been chatting on Snapchat (ew!) but they were now about to finally meet in the flesh. Which, just to be clear,

I WOULD NEVER DO IN REAL LIFE.

Ever since I was zero, even before I could walk, talk, tie my shoelaces and definitely before I had a phone, my parents have warned me against meeting up with people I've met online. I've had it etched into my brain like hieroglyphics into stone. And even though this was all pretend, it still felt wrong. But you gotta do what you gotta do, right?

So, pretend Ana in pretend diary is nervous about meeting pretend Tennyson. Nervous about telling him that she's dying. Nervous about her appearance. Will she/won't she wear a wig?

I've got to say, this pretend diary is a page turner. If I wasn't writing it, I wouldn't be able to put it down. The diary ends with some very specific detail.

About where and when Ana and Tennyson will meet: 3.30 pm on Thursday at the Blue Turtle café, around the corner from the school.

Here's the important part of the plan. My last lesson on Thursday is History. The only class I share with Butt Breath. I make sure that I sit next to her in class that day (urghhh, but no pain, no gain) and I 'accidentally' leave the pretend diary behind when the bell goes.

I bolt at the sound of the bell, momentarily stopping at the door to see if Alyssa's noticed the diary. Sure enough, she's slipping it into her bag. It's almost boring how predictably evil she is. She has a sinister smirk on her face, obviously pretty chuffed with herself.

I make my way to the Blue Turtle where Al is waiting for me. So far, it's all going according to plan. I sit at a table by myself. Waiting for pretend boy to arrive. Al sits at a table at the back of the café and texts me.

Holy hole in a doughnut, Ana . . . she's live-streaming about your 'hook-up' on Insta. And she's on her way here now.

Are you recording it?

I'm on it.

He gives me the thumbs-up from afar. Butt Breath arrives at the café but hides outside. I can hear her talking to her followers about this 'live dud date' and how funny it is. I wait for pretend Tennyson. He doesn't come, of course. I pretend to look outside. I pretend to be sad.

Al sends me another message.

Oscar-worthy performance!

Some time goes by. Tennyson doesn't show up. I bury my head in my hands and slump forward on the table. Alyssa finally enters the café and shoves her phone camera in my face.

'What's the matter, Ana? You look all sad and . . . lonely. Were you expecting someone? A boyfriend, perhaps?'

Aaaaand CUT!

I won't bore you with the rest of the scene. Suffice to say, I cried crocodile tears and Alyssa lapped it all up. She laughed. She mocked me. She made me wave to her online followers. And Al recorded it all.

Mission accomplished.

Phase 2 – Gathering evidence

Al called a meeting to review our evidence. Measure it up against other cases that had been before the courts. We wanted a watertight case. Laws vary in different countries and even from state to state in the same country so it's hard to know for sure, but from the limited research that can be done online by two 12.5-year-olds, it seemed that we had a pretty solid case of cyberbullying. The video footage was additional evidence to support the online material.

We were pretty close to being ready. Ready to take this to the police and file a complaint against Butt Breath. But before that, we had other things to consider. For starters, I had to tell my parents. Somehow, I had managed to keep the whole Alyssa saga to myself all these years. The punch was the first they knew about anything being wrong. They assumed I had overreacted to some random bully because I was going through so much with the cancer and everything.

You see, that's the thing about being bullied. It comes with shame. It really shouldn't, and deep in my heart, I know that. But that doesn't change the fact that somehow in some warped, twisted way, I thought that this was all my fault. That somehow, I must deserve to be treated so badly. If I was stronger, I'd fight back, I'd tell somebody, I'd make it stop. But in all these years, I hadn't even managed to do the simplest thing of all. Tell Mum and Dad.

Part of me didn't want to worry or alarm them. I didn't want them to be heartbroken about their kid being a target at school. They have always loved and supported me so much. How could I do this to them?

Another part of me simply felt embarrassed. Would they think I was weak for not putting a stop to it? And the longer it went on, the harder it was to say anything. In those early days, I contemplated telling them, especially when Butt Breath started spitting on me when I got off the bus. But I never quite found the courage. Yet here I was, with less than a year to live, finding myself with more courage than I've ever had in my life. Death has a way of doing that to you.

So, the time had come. I called a family meeting. I'd asked Mum to come over to Dad and Wanda's so that I could tell them all at once. I also asked Al to come along. After all, he was my partner in crime.

Devastation sweeps the land

'Since Year 5?! This has been going on for years and you haven't told us?' Mum was mortified.

As was Dad. 'Oh, Ana Banana, I'm so sorry. Why didn't you say something before?'

Wanda was in top form, as usual. 'You should've punched her TWICE in the noggin. That little witch!'

I wasn't sure what they were more rattled by. The fact that I'd been bullied for so long, or that I hadn't told them about it. Either way, it was pretty hard to watch them absorb this news. It was hard to see them so devastated. And so I did what I always do in these situations – I checked out. Not on purpose, of course. I don't make a conscious decision to go on brain breaks. They just happen. So, my memory of the rest of that meeting is a little hazy. If it were to be distilled into a sprinkling of words, it would look something like this:

Unconscionable

Counsellor

WHY?

KIDS Helpline

Are you Okay?

HOW?

Justice

Nasty

Sociopath

EGO

Unbelievable

Want me to break her legs?

EVERYONE: WANDA!

We fully support you

psychologist

Ms LONGBOTTOM

SO SORRY

HARASSMENT

WE LOVE YOU

When I came back from my brain break, I realised that Al had been filling in the gaps. While I was trying to mentally hitchhike to way, way out where the buses don't run, Al was fielding questions from my folks and showing them the investigative work we'd been doing in order to bring Alyssa to justice with the law. The upshot of all this was that my parents, after going on an emotional roller-coaster and being horrified by the evidence of the online cruelty, were fully on board with filing a complaint to the police.

So that was that. It was done. Phase 2 complete.

And breathe . . .

It felt good to breathe.

Come on, do it with me.

Breathe in . . .

And out . . .

For a brief moment, I could just sit back and relax. The hardest part was yet to come but I was happy knowing that for now, things were in place. Or to use Dad's corny phrase, 'all my ducks were in a row'.

Al and I took a detour from our road to justice and stopped off for some ice-cream. Literally. Not metaphorically this time.

I'm talking triple scoop – tiramisu, lemon and liquorice. Don't judge me. You have your weird flavour combos and I have mine. That afternoon was strangely therapeutic. Al made me play one of his many frustrating, hypothetical games. This one was his favourite and it was called . . .

Would you rather

'Would you rather sing everything you say or rap everything you say?'

I went with rap as I'm a terrible singer. Cannot hold a tune. I'm not being modest. You should hear me sing. All kinds of bad.

'Would you rather have loud, annoying hiccups that never, ever go away, or have to always give wedgies to anyone wearing yellow pants?'

You'll be surprised, but I went with the wedgie option. Hiccups are the worst! And yellow pants are not that common. Relatively easy choice, I thought.

The next one was a toughie.

'Would you rather wear your swimmers in public every single day or do just one lap of an Olympic-sized pool filled with spew?'

I gagged. 'Ewwww!'

Al looked at me deadpan. 'Choose.'

'Backstroke or freestyle?'

'Backstroke.'

I chose spew. Swimmers in the streets were just not an option. Nup.

After we finished our ice-creams and Al was done

quizzing me about all kinds of absurd and impossible situations, we headed home. By then, Mum, Dad and Wanda had recovered from the shock of all that I had dumped on them and we all managed to have a nice, calm dinner together. Al stayed, of course, and I even asked Plastic Pat to join us. Mum was particularly happy about that. Listen, I don't really *dis*like Pat. I just think he's a

boofhead.

A boofhead who makes Mum happy for some reason. So, I do what any gold-star, above-and-beyond, champion daughter would do – just suck it up. You can't love all the choices your parents make. But you can live and let live. And that's what I'm doing.

Wanda cooked rice and some mushy casserole thing that looked more like baby poo than anything that should go in your mouth. It didn't smell too appetising either. We all hesitated when she plonked the pot in the middle of the table. Even Al, who loves just about any kind of cuisine, looked horrified. You could feel the tension in the air as everyone slowly leaned in for a closer look and a ***whiff*** of the food. You could almost see the cogs turning in their minds – at phenomenal speed. How should they respond to this giant dish of brown slime?

Pat was the first to speak. 'Wow. What do you call this?'

Dad jumped in, panicked. 'It looks spectacular, darling!'

Apparently it was cauliflower and fish stew. She'd found the recipe in one of those trashy women's magazines and thought it looked good. But even Wanda herself was having trouble holding back her gag reflex as she served up her new dish . . . 'Monkfish Chowder'.

Nobody said anything. We all dug our spoons bravely into the goo. It didn't taste as putrid as it looked and smelled. But it was obvious that we were all jealous of what the smaller kids were eating. Chicken nuggets, BBQ sauce and packet mash.

Monkfish Chowder aside, I think this was the first time that my whole family - and I mean my WHOLE family, right down to Spanx, Kim and Kanye, had ever shared a meal. And it was surprisingly pleasant. We were like the Brady Bunch - on steroids. I realised during that unconventional, fish-stenchy dinner that I was, in fact, one of the luckiest girls in the world. Who else has a team of people as big as this on their side? Sure, they're kooky and some of them can't yet form full sentences but they all support me **100** percent. Mum, Dad and Al would walk through a house fire for me and the others are close behind. Including Plastic Pat, who was being more supportive than ever. I had a team. My very own posse. And they were going to see me through this brilliant revenge (ahem, I mean JUSTICE) plan.

Spanner in the works

As with all things in life – or death – the best-laid plans don't always work out. The police, Alyssa and justice would have to wait, because my illness took a turn for the worse. The cancer had spread to more lymph nodes. Everyone was surprised by these results as I had seemed to be responding well to the chemo. I had been bouncing back. For weeks now, I had been fully functional. No days off school. Appetite in check. Energy levels good. The hair situation was still patchy but I had my wigs. I had thought I was adjusting to my 'new normal' pretty well, and some days I even allowed myself to think that I could beat this thing. That maybe I was in that small percentage of people who fully recovered. I mean, why wouldn't I be? *Somebody* had to be in that tiny, exclusive club of survivors, right? Why not me? I was young, fit and positive. That's why my sudden turn for the worse came as a shock. Almost as soon as we got the news that the cancer had spread, I became too sick to go to school. Too sick to even go to hospital. Ekua started coming to our house to give me treatment.

Mum and Dad decided that I should stay in one place for the time being. And since my dad's place was overcrowded, I would stay with Mum. But Dad spent most of his time with me, at Mum's. He would sit in the armchair next to my bed and read to me.

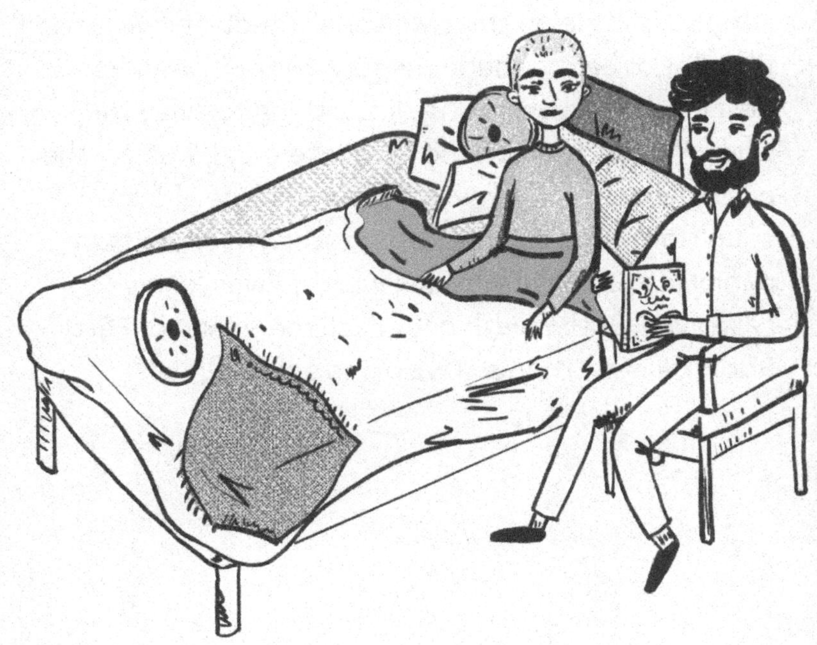

Not your conventional books for kids my age, either. No *Harry Potter* or *Baby-Sitters Club*. The first book he read to me was *Persepolis* – a graphic novel by an Iranian author who grew up in Iran during the Islamic revolution. I loved it. And I loved the fact that my dad was so devoted to teaching me about my Iranian heritage. Even though he's not the Iranian parent in this equation.

Mum would check in on us regularly. She'd bring cups of tea for Dad and all sorts of treats and snacks for me, in the hope that I'd eat something. But I couldn't. I just couldn't face food. Me and food had become like oil and water. Like Taylor Swift and Kanye West. Never the twain shall meet. The very thought of eating made me gag. Even my mum's delicious Persian cooking did nothing to sway me. Chelo-kebab, my all-time favourite meal, was off the cards. I would force myself to have some chicken soup from time to time, just to stop my mum from panicking about how much weight I was losing.

No way Butt Breath could call me Porkie or Fatty Boomba now. Though I wish she could.

I MISSED MY CURVES.

I ALSO MISSED MY HAIR.

I MISSED HAVING THE ENERGY TO DANCE. AND PLAY. AND MAKE REVENGE PLANS.

I MISSED BEING ME.

This new version of me was different. Cancer had stuck its ugly claws into every part of my life. Not just the stuff you see, but the stuff you don't see. Like my optimism. My will to fight this jerk-bag of a disease.

I had hit a new low and wasn't sure how I'd find the way back up. I needed someone to throw me a lifeline.

Trial and error

Dr Needham told us about a clinical trial that I could try. Some new experimental path that might help my chances of survival. I didn't really understand what this trial would involve. Only that some world-leading paediatric oncologist (aka kid-cancer doc) from the Children's Hospital of Philadelphia was doing it. She had come up with some new immune therapy that seemed to work rapidly with the type of cancer that I had. Don't ask me the name of it. Something, something T-cell therapy.

Clinical trials are not a guarantee. Nowhere near it. In fact, I'm pretty sure we had to sign a bunch of papers to say we accepted the fact that it might not work and could in fact be a colossal waste of our time and money. But when you've tried everything else and you're still sliding down that dreaded cancer slippery-dip, you think, 'Why not?'

Mum and Dad were very keen. Mum has always been interested in anything on the fringe. Any new and wondrous path. She's a big believer in humans overcoming the greatest challenges. Making the impossible possible.

'If we sent a man to the moon in 1969, then surely 50-something years on we can find a cure for cancer.'

She is the eternal optimist. And Dad, despite his innate cynicism, was also feeling positive about the new trial. The only catch was that I couldn't have the treatment here at home. I had to go to America. My parents decided that Mum and I would go and Dad would stay back. I knew he was sad about that but he had too many responsibilities here.

The next few days were hectic. Flying halfway across the world at such short notice requires some serious organisational skills. Mum did all the boring things like booking flights and getting our visas and medical papers sorted and Dad spent every waking moment with me. Reading to me, beating me at chess (don't tell him but I let him win) and just hanging out.

I was nervous about the trial. I didn't want to get my hopes up but I couldn't help it. Just thinking about the possibility of this new magical wonder-treatment curing me lifted my spirits. Hope is a phenomenal medicine.

I said goodbye to Al.

'Eat all the hotdogs!'

'*All* of them?'

'They have every kind of dog you can imagine! Bacon dog, nacho dog, corn dog, chili dog, onion

dog and the Monte Cristo dog. That baby has ham, turkey, Swiss cheese AND maple syrup on it.'

'Ew!'

'Did you know that it was originally a German dude who introduced hotdogs to America? He was a street vendor who sold sausages. A German sausage called the dachshund. Get it? Dachshund, like the dog? Anyway, the sausages were too hot to hold and would burn people's hands. They were literally HOT dogs. So, he started giving out gloves to protect people's fingers, but the gloves never got returned. Then his wife said, "Hey, why don't we put the dachshund in a bun!" Except she probably said it in German. And that's how the hotdog came to be.' Al came up momentarily for air. Then he continued, 'I have no idea if any of that is true but it sounds legit.'

It was typical of Al to google American food before anything else. I think he's going to be a food critic when he grows up. Except he won't actually criticise anything because he loves all food. Any food. Any time of the day. He's what you call a 'foodie'.

I also said goodbye to Dad. Which wasn't easy. I was only going to be gone for a month but he hugged me like he was never going to see me again. Wanda kissed me on the forehead and slipped me a couple of hundred-dollar notes. She told me to buy something lush and entirely unnecessary. It was a big deal for her to give me all that cash. She and Dad weren't made of money so I knew what a sacrifice it must've been. I decided then and there that I was going to buy a pair of Jordan 1s. High tops, of course. I had wanted a pair of those for a long time.

US of A

So off we went.

To America.

The land of hotdogs, guns and cutting-edge medical trials. It wasn't exactly a fun trip. No stops at Disneyland or the Grand Canyon. No climbing to the top of the Empire State Building or skipping along the stars on Hollywood Boulevard. Maybe I'd get to do that on another trip. When I was all healed and whole and my cancer was a thing of the past.

Or maybe not. Maybe I'd never see a Broadway show or eat a buffalo wing in Buffalo. I certainly wouldn't be doing any of that this time. This was a short, intense visit to the Children's Hospital of Philadelphia where they hooked me up to machines and drugged me up for 30 days straight. But it wasn't as bad as it sounds. The Americans were super nice. Super helpful. Super enthusiastic.

It was super weird.

They're like a whole other breed of humans who have been injected with some kind of positivity potion. It was both wonderful and exhausting at the same time. We stayed in a lovely cancer ward. A lot nicer than my hospital back home. I don't know if it was because this was a well-known children's hospital or if we were in a particularly nice ward, but

I loved the feel of this place. No fluoro lights or stark white walls. Nope. This place had colours. Bright furniture. Flowers on every desk and just a general warm glow that made you feel safe and relaxed.

Every day for half an hour, Mum and I would go for a walk along the cobblestone streets nearby. It was charming and ye olde. I was pretty worn out and weak from the medication so we'd take it slow. Very slow. Mum thought this was a good thing. My whole life, she'd been telling me to 'stop and smell the roses' and here we were, doing just that. It was spring and beautiful blossoms surrounded us wherever we went. These were precious times. I was happy. Perfectly content. Somehow not worried about how the trial would turn out or whether I'd live till my next birthday, or even about Alyssa. As if by magic, and just for those few weeks, I just didn't care about those things anymore.

And I made a friend. Her name was Kenya and she was exactly one year (to the day) older than me. She too had Non-Hodgkin's lymphoma but her health was much worse than mine. She was in pain which was something I hadn't experienced yet. They'd give her morphine if it got really bad.

And sometimes her breathing got heavy and fast so she'd have to use an oxygen cylinder to help regulate it. But she didn't let any of that kill her joy. She was fiercely funny and really good to be around and she insisted on calling me by my full and proper name. Anahita. We spent so much time together. Talking, playing cards, watching Netflix or snoozing in adjacent beds.

Kenya's family were from Kenya. Though she was born and bred in Philly, like the Fresh Prince. She was the very definition of cool. Even while wearing a hospital gown and hooked up to a thousand tubes and machines, she still had sass.

> **Sassy (*sa-si*)**
> *Adjective, informal*
> **Stylish, chic, self-assured, spirited, bold. If you threw Lizzo, Lady Gaga, Serena Williams and Judge Judy into a blender, you'd get a sass-smoothie. You'd get Kenya.**

She was a straight shooter. No beating around the bush. No sugar-coating our reality. We had cancer. We were most likely going to die. And that was okay.

Her view had a different twist. She saw our problem as being a mathematical one. Everybody got an allotted number. The number of years they got to roam the earth.

36

78.6

(average female life expectancy)

6

22

17

With 122 being the most anyone has ever got – according to the *Guinness World Records*. That ancient lady would've outlived her kids *and* her grandkids!

'It's a numbers game,' said Kenya, 'and let's face it, you and me are getting scammed. If you go by the average, then we're probably looking at a six to one ratio.'

I'm usually good with numbers but it took me a while to get my head around this equation. Or how counting years and dividing them into ratios affected our day-to-day reality. Kenya explained, 'It's simple. For every six days that other kids get, we get one. So, we can either moan and groan about it or we can . . .

CRAM
IT
ALL IN

Basically, we were in a race against time. We had to live our lives to the max. No time to waste. Not even a second. Death was waiting for us. Like an eager bouncer at the door of the world's most feared club. And there were things to be done before we would step across that threshold, into the abyss.

I loved Kenya's attitude. She was keen-beans, positive and upbeat. How did she do it? I wished I could bottle up some of her enthusiasm and inject it into my veins with the next dose of my trial meds. It's not that I *didn't* want to cram it all in - but making it my mission felt like a lot of pressure. Some days I just wanted to veg out. Do nothing. Zip. Zero. I wanted to be allowed the luxury of being bored. And sick. And ordinary. It wasn't fair that other kids got to faff about and waste time and I didn't. Why did it all have to count? Why was my life under a microscope while others went about their business without a care?

Kenya acknowledged that these were fair questions but we didn't have time to delve into them right now. In fact, we didn't have time, full stop. We had things to do. Things like eating a Philly cheesesteak.

A what?

She was mortified by the fact that I had never heard of the famous Philly cheesesteak. And that

I wasn't really keen to try it. Kenya was having none of that. So, on one of our afternoons off from treatment, we got special permission for her to take her oxygen tank out of the hospital and she and her dad took Mum and I to the most famous cheesesteak joint in Philadelphia – Geno's Steaks. The line for this place snaked all the way down the street and around the corner. I was baffled by the fact that these people were all lining up to eat what was seemingly a white bread roll with fried meat and cheese inside. While we waited in line, we made small talk . . . and **big** talk (is that a thing?). We had epiphanies and belly laughs and Kenya's dad schooled me on the ins and outs of ordering a cheesesteak. There was a very specific way to order. You had to get it right otherwise you'd look like a tourist and nobody wanted that. There were three cheeses to choose from: Whiz, American or Provolone. And there was the option of fried onions. You could either have it 'wit' onions or 'wit-out'. Both were respectable choices. When ordering, you were NOT to say the word 'Philly' or 'cheesesteak'. Those were implied. So, depending on what you wanted to order, you would simply say something like 'whiz wit' or 'prov wit-out'. Ordering a sandwich had never felt more stressful! After 35 minutes of waiting and careful ordering (I opted for 'whiz wit-out'), we had our cheesesteaks and it was time to dig in. S'cuse the pun, but the 'stakes' were high. I felt enormous pressure to like this greasy hot sandwich. Kenya had put so much love and effort into this excursion. It's okay, I thought to myself. Even if I hated it, I'd fake it. I'd pretend it was delicious. Sometimes you have to fake things for the greater good. Or to spare someone's feelings.

So, I took a deep breath and bit into it. And . . .

IT. WAS. AMA-ZING.

Not even lying, you guys. No fake news here. Swear to Queen Bey herself, this combination of gritty meat, stiff crusty bread and fluorescent yellow cheese, which looked like something that was manufactured in a nuclear power plant, was a gift from the heavens. Sandwich wizardry. Something I should have had on my bucket list if only I'd known it existed. Now, thanks to Kenya . . . tick!

A few weeks ago, I could barely hold down a spoonful of soup and now I was chowing down on cheesesteaks with my new friend on the other side of the planet. I told Kenya that once she got better, she'd have to fly to Oz and I'd introduce her to the meat pie – which has nothing on the cheesesteak but it's all we've got. She agreed. I thanked Kenya and her dad for what was truly one of the best afternoons of my life. Life's ups and downs sure had a way of surprising me. Even when I think I know what's coming next, I don't.

Honestly, I could never have foreseen this friendship. Or feeling this good. Perhaps whatever magical drugs they were injecting me with in this trial were working? Perhaps we'd all be okay.

Perhaps,

perhaps,

perhaps.

Doctor Who?

So, the team of a billion doctors did their thing. I saw so many different specialists that they started to become interchangeable and blend into one.

Mum had countless meetings with them. They seemed pleased with how I was progressing, but no one had any definitive answers. We just had to wait and see. So, eventually, the trial was over and it was time for us to go home.

I said goodbye to all the super-duper-positive American docs and nurses.

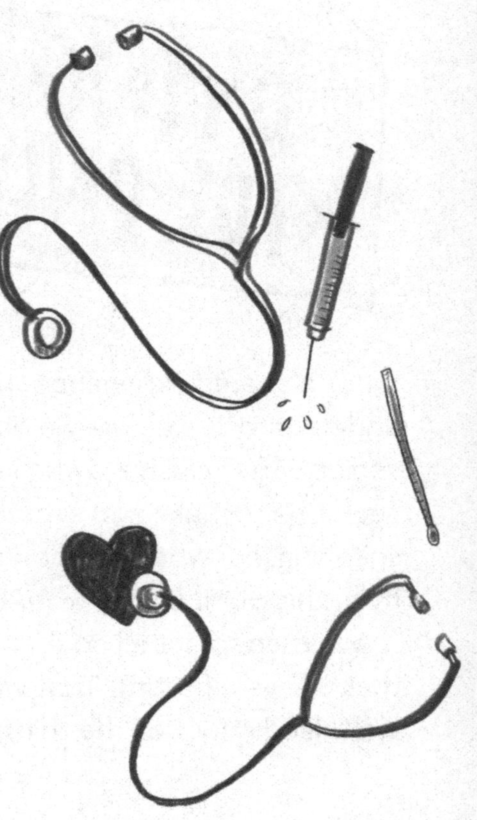

I said goodbye to Kenya.

That goodbye felt like a kick in the gut. It was strange how cosmically connected we had become in such a short time. Four weeks ago we hadn't even met and yet now she was my kindred spirit. One month felt like ten years. But in a good way. Kenya and I *got* each other. We had an unspoken language, a shared experience that no one else really understood. It was like we belonged to a secret society. An exclusive 'dying kids' club with its own secret handshake and everything. Geographically speaking, our worlds couldn't be further apart, but from this point on, we would always be sisters.

We tried to act all cool. Like it was no biggie that we were parting. That we'd see each other again. We talked about all the things we'd do when we did

DYING KIDS ONLY

catch up but somehow, deep in our hearts, we knew that this goodbye would be forever. Even if we both survived the cancer, the chances of us eating a meat pie together anytime soon were slim to none. My mum fought back tears as I hugged Kenya. Seeing her cry made me cry too and it set off a chain reaction. Before long, Mum, me, Kenya and Kenya's dad were all a snotty-nosed mess, wiping our tears away with our sleeves.

Somebody get me off this roller-coaster of emotions already!

Goodbye, sunny Philadelphia, I'll never forget these bittersweet days.

Next stop – home sweet home.

Business as usual

Not long after our return, I started to feel better. Not bouncing off the walls better but well enough to return to school. And, as Al dutifully pointed out, well enough to execute the final stages of the revenge plan. But now, I was a bit ambivalent about revenge. So much had happened in such a short time. And to be honest, I wasn't sure if I could be bothered wasting all that time and energy going to the police and pressing charges against Alyssa. Mum and Dad felt differently. They were not going to let this slide. As far as they were concerned, Alyssa's bullying was not only cruel but criminal and it had to be dealt with, no matter what. I agreed but I just wasn't up to it right now. I managed to convince them to delay it for a little while. At least till I got over the jet-lag! So, the revenge plan went on the backburner . . .

. . . until my first day back at school, when I was greeted by this:

ALYSSA: 'YOU LOOK LIKE A LIVING TRASH FIRE, GIRL. WHAT DID THEY DO TO YOU OVER THERE? INJECT YOU WITH MORE CANCER?'

I looked at Al.

He gave me a knowing nod.

We were back on.

Taking Alyssa down had once again jumped to the top of my to-do list. That afternoon, as I was messaging Kenya and updating her on the Butt Breath situation, Al showed up at my house. Unannounced.

'What is this, a drop-in? How'd you know I'd be home?'

'You're always home. Tell your mum we're going for a walk.'

I didn't feel like going for a walk but Al was eager, in a way I'd never seen before. He seemed distracted. His mind was racing. He insisted that I go. As we left the house, he typed an address into Google Maps on his phone and led the way. He was walking fast. I struggled to keep up.

'Where are we going?'

He told me to just shoosh and follow, but I was too tired and too curious.

'Slow down! And tell me where we're going.'

'Stop with the twenty questions already.'

'You stop being so mysterious!'

'Just walk, Ana. One foot in front of the other. You'll find out soon.'

'You're infuriating!'

'In-furi-what? Sounds like a compliment. Is it?'

'Urrghhhhh!'

'You always use big words. Did you know that?'

'TELL ME WHERE WE'RE GOING, AL!'

'Okay, okay! Keep your wig on. I'll tell you, but only if you promise to still come.'

What was he up to? I promised him that I would still go, but he made me put my hand on my heart and swear on Kim and Kanye's lives. I said that I could take or leave those two furry mutts but I would keep my word. And then he told me . . .

'We're going to Alyssa's house.'

I turned back immediately. No way. What am I, crazy? Al grabbed my arm and begged me to trust him. He told me that he had followed Alyssa home after school today because he wanted to confront her about me and when he got there, he discovered something. Something I should know about.

'What? Why don't you just tell me?

Why do you have to drag me all the way to her house?'

But that's not how it was going to work. Not today. Apparently, I had to see it for myself. So, I followed Al along the curvy backstreets of my suburb, imagining all sorts of scenarios awaiting me.

Butt Breath reclining on her designer leather chair, stroking her white cat and poking needles into voodoo dolls of me.

Or her polishing her broom and dusting off her pointy black hat, confirming my belief that she's actually a real-life witch.

But nothing prepared me for what I was actually about to see. When we arrived, Al dragged me through the bushes in the front garden so that we'd get closer to the house itself. We were officially trespassing but he didn't seem to care.

'You're just not going to believe this.'

For a guy who usually can't stop talking, he was remarkably quiet about whatever it was he wanted to show me. A thorn scratched my leg as we crept up between the rosebushes surrounding Alyssa's front door.

'This is possibly the weirdest thing you've ever done, Al. And you've done some WEIRD things in your day.'

He just laughed in response as we edged closer and closer to Alyssa's exquisite arched yellow front door.

'Are we actually going into her house? Please tell me you're not about to knock on the door?'

Al said nothing.

'Jeeeez, Al, give me something. What are we doing here?'

Finally, he stopped. He took my hand in his, looked at me with calm, serene eyes and pointed to the window next to the front door. The blinds were drawn but there was a gap through which we could peer inside.

Behind closed doors

I will only describe what I saw. I will not try to put into words my feelings about what I saw.

Alyssa was feeding a guy.

He was in a wheelchair.

He was young. Probably still a teenager.

He was hooked up to a machine. Tubes everywhere.

She was feeding him some kind of gooey porridge thing. She was gentle with him. Wiping his mouth after each spoonful of goo. And she talked to him, even though he didn't respond. Not even with facial expressions. He was catatonic.

> **Catatonic (*kat-uh-ton-ik*)**
> *Adjective*
> Unresponsive. Appearing to be in a daze or stupor. Like one of those zombies from *The Return of the Living Dead*, moments before they pounce.

He couldn't do anything for himself.

Alyssa was his carer.

Second life

All that I knew, or thought I knew about Alyssa Anderson, was suddenly tipped upside down. I wanted to leave, to get as far away from her house as I possibly could, but my feet were cemented. I looked at Al. He looked at me. There was not much either of us could say. We both stayed and spied through the window as she finished feeding the young guy, adjusted his seat, fluffed up his pillow to make him more comfortable, then picked up a book and started reading it to him.

I finally stepped back.

I'd seen enough.

Without saying a word to each other, Al and I started to walk back to my house. We walked in silence for the longest time. I tried to process my feelings. Tried to make sense of what I'd seen. This wasn't the same Butt Breath who had been tormenting me for most of my childhood.

Well, it *was* her, but it wasn't.

This Alyssa was kind. Long-suffering. It was obvious from the practised way she was doing things that she'd been looking after this guy for a long time. This was her other reality. This was her second life. The flipside of the Alyssa Anderson coin.

She was human after all.

I felt a surge of emotions. A roller-coaster of conflicting feelings. I was both relieved and resentful. If she's capable of compassion, then why was she so cruel to me? Maybe she had to compartmentalise her life to survive. Maybe life at home was so unbearable that she had to be nasty to me to relieve the pressure? Maybe she's a proper Jekyll and Hyde? You know, a split personality. None of it made sense. If the evil villainous Butt Breath was actually Mother Teresa at home, then where did that leave me?

Al finally broke the silence.

'How's that for a mind *pffrrroooarrrr*?!' He made an explosive sound and a mind-exploding hand gesture.

'Yeah,' was about all I could say.

'It kinda changes everything, doesn't it?'

He was right. There was no way we could press charges now. As horrid as Alyssa had been and continued to be, her life obviously sucked and getting the police involved wasn't going to help anyone.

'She's still a cow,' I said, feeling betrayed by this new image of a caring, self-sacrificing Alyssa.

'Totally,' agreed Al. 'Do ya reckon it's possible for someone to be both good and evil at the same time?'

'I guess,' I replied. There wasn't a whole lot more to be said after that. We walked quietly, kicking the same rock back and forth between us all the way home.

Mr K

Fast forward three weeks. Three weeks of mental gymnastics. I bent my mind every which way in a desperate attempt to comprehend this dual reality. Butt Breath Anderson – supervillain *and* superhero? But I failed miserably. Mind would not compute. There was an error in the system. If only I could turn the world off and then restart it. Maybe then I could escape The Upside Down, this whacky alternate dimension, and everything would make sense.

While my mind was doing backflips, my body was behaving well. Like a champion, in fact. Seemed like the 'good cells' were throwing some heavy punches in the ring, making Dr Needham and my parents very happy. Of course, there were still no guarantees. The trial therapy was working well so far and we were hopeful that it might prolong my life. But that hope was flimsy. Nobody was making any grand promises. Still, flimsy hope is better than no hope. You take what you can get when you're battling the big C.

Getting back to my nemesis. In light of the revelation regarding Butt Breath's home situation, Mum, Dad and I decided the police route wasn't the best option. Instead, we thought the best way to try and resolve the ongoing bullying issue was to involve the school counsellor, Mr Kendrick.

Mr K, as he likes to be called, is a very short, buff man. You've never seen anyone with so much muscle. His hair is always immaculate. And he dresses like he's just about to shoot a cover for *Vogue*. His sense of style makes him stand out in a suburban high school where most teachers look tired and worn out. And he has an unusually high voice, which is startling when you first hear him speak. The mega muscles combined with the Mickey Mouse voice does throw you a bit. But you get used to it. Mr K is tough and uncompromising when it comes to the school rules but he's got a heart as spacious as the universe. He knows each and every student by name and genuinely cares about ALL of us.

HE CARES ABOUT . . .

THE COOL KIDS

. . . 'SUP

WHAT A NOOB!

THE GEEKS

COME AT ME, BRO!

THUGS

. . .
$\cos(\pi - \alpha) = -\cos\alpha$
. . .

NERDS

. . . LIFE IS BUT A WALKING SHADOW . . .

EMOS

WHAT IF 'WHY' WASN'T A WORD? COULD YOU STILL ASK QUESTIONS?

MISFITS

No matter who they are, the kids always greet him with a high five or a 'K-man!', or they stop for a 'hang'n'chat'. When he's on yard duty everyone flocks to him. He's never avoided and alone like the other teachers.

We told Mr K what I'd seen at Alyssa's house but of course he already knew. Apparently her brother Max had been in a terrible car accident when he was fourteen. Alyssa's mum, who was driving, had died instantly. Leaving Alyssa and her dad to look after Max. Her dad worked long hours so they had a nurse who cared for Max during the day. But when Alyssa got home from school, she took over.

This had been her reality since I met her. And I never knew.

Nobody knew. Except Mr K and some of the teachers. It made me wonder about all the things people keep hidden. How many deep, dark secrets linger behind closed doors?

It broke my heart. It really did. It made me want to just forget about the past and give her a hug. I wanted to tell her that I forgave her. That I could see her pain. That life had been cruel to her just as it had been cruel to me. I wanted to tell her that I would be her friend. That she could count on me.

But how would I do it? Since 'the punch', she had gone back to being openly mean. Back to spitting on me when I got off the bus. To posting horrible things about me online. She would yell 'Fatty Boomba' when she'd see me across the schoolyard, even though I was obviously underweight these days. As horrible as her behaviour still made me feel, she was now doing more damage to herself than me. You see, before people knew I had cancer, they just witnessed the abuse and shrugged it off as part of high school life. A sad cliché. I'm not saying that kids approved of the bullying, but for the most part, they were probably just glad it wasn't aimed at them. It's called the 'bystander' effect. No one was willing to risk Alyssa's wrath by interfering or sticking up for me. Al was an exception, of course. He always said something clumsy and sweet in my defence.

'Do you ever take a day off from being a

meany jerk-face bum?!'

His insults only made Alyssa laugh. Which was not the desired effect.

But now things had changed. Even the most indifferent person couldn't stand by and watch her sling ugly words at me, like she had a million times before, without feeling something. If you said nothing as someone harassed 'the dying girl', then you were heartless. And most people weren't heartless. So, this latest round of taunts and torture was backfiring on Alyssa. Kids were now sticking up for me. Nothing dramatic or earth-shattering, but they were telling her to shut up. And back off. To get a life.

None of that stopped her, though.

Restorative justice

Mr K suggested 'restorative justice'. It's what all the hip schools do now to resolve bullying and harassment issues. According to this model, I had three options.

1. **Face Alyssa and try to resolve the problem one on one. I wasn't to bring in emotions and say things like 'You made me feel x, y or z' because that makes people defensive. I was to say 'How did this all start? What happened? What can you do to repair what's been happening?'**

2. **We'd deal with it in the classroom. The teacher would talk about bullying to the whole class but use an example that was very direct and specific to what Alyssa had been doing to me. So that she'd know what we were talking about but no one else would. (This option was good in theory but would never work because**

you'd have to be living under a rock to not know this was being directed at Butt Breath. There were no other bullies of her calibre in these parts. She owned that crown.)

3. **Mediation. Not to be confused with meditation . . .**

OMMMMMM!

MEDIATION is basically a friendly confrontation. We'd have Mr K, Alyssa, her dad and my folks all sit around and talk it out. This would allow me the opportunity to talk about my feelings and how Butt Breath's actions had caused me pain.

I didn't have to think long about what I wanted to do. I knew in my gut that I had to take Option 1 and face Alyssa. She'd terrorised me for years but I wasn't afraid anymore. I felt sorry for her. I had to do this. I was dying. Who knew how much longer I had to live. I didn't want to chicken out of this and regret it in the next world.

Bad to worse

When it rains, it pours. And right now it was bucketing down. Just when I thought life couldn't get any more complicated, I got the news.

I had been messaging Kenya about all the twists and turns in the soap opera that is my life. We'd WhatsApp each other a hundred times a day. Mum and Dad made fun of the constant *ding ding ding* alerting me to new messages from Kenya. But for three whole days now, she hadn't responded to anything. I could see that she hadn't even seen my messages. I tried connecting with her on Insta but she was totally offline. I assumed that she'd gone in for some emergency treatment and had no access to her phone.

What I didn't assume was that she had died.

So, when Mum came into my room late one night, looking as pale as a ghost, I knew that something bad had happened. It took her a long time to find the words but eventually she managed. She had just received an email from the head oncologist from our trial. She knew that Kenya and I had become close, so she wanted to let us know personally. Kenya had become progressively worse in the weeks after the trial and had passed away peacefully three days ago.

I was gutted.

Passed away.
Slipped away.
Transitioned.
Departed.
Dead.

I had only spent four earthly weeks with Kenya but she was my soul sister. An instant best friend. Just add chemo! The pain of losing her was all-consuming. She was gone.

Gone.

I kept scrolling through our messages. She was JUST here. Her last message was sent three days ago at 7.12 am. How could she have simply vanished?

Of course, that's a silly question. I've spent this whole book talking about death and coming to terms with it. But somehow it's different when you're at the heart of all the attention. I had spent so much time trying to prepare others for my big farewell that I hadn't thought about how losing someone close would feel like to me.

It was horrible. I cried and cried. I skipped school for pretty much the whole week. I wrote a card and sent it to Kenya's family. I asked Mum to print out the photos we took when we were together. I've pinned my favourite one on my wall. Taken at Genc's Steaks, of course.

I lay in bed
for days, crying
and reading. Trying to distract my mind from the enormity of life and death. Would I be seeing Kenya soon? Would she be there to greet me when my time came? Could she travel through dimensions and visit me in my dreams?

Tell me what it's like over there, Kenya. Tell me.

Is it comfy? Like walking barefoot on cushiony

clouds? Can you still see us down here? Struggling and fighting to live an earthly life? Does it all seem ridiculous now that you're in heaven?

I kept on with the questions. Even though I couldn't hear her answers, I somehow knew that she could hear me. She was right here. Next to me. Untouchable. Invisible. But close. Closer than my own life vein. I couldn't explain the feeling. It wasn't logical. But I knew it to be true.

Tell me, Kenya. Is there a Geno's up there? An even better (if that is at all possible) heavenly version? What about other foods - dumplings, tiramisu, fried chicken? Surely there has to be. What's heaven without good eats?

And is it crowded? A mosh pit of souls? I mean, if every single person who has ever walked the earth is now up there, it's gotta be jam-packed. And do you just get to meet whoever you want, from whenever? Like Shakespeare, Mahatma Gandhi or Prince? Is he singing 'Purple Rain' up there above the cushiony clouds?

Tell me, Kenya. Tell me everything. But most of all, tell me this - are you happy?

She never replied. Not in words, anyway.

Which suited me fine. Why ruin a perfectly good conversation with words? She spoke to me in a different way. In a trippy, mystical way. She sent me calm. Calm that would wrap itself around me like a weighted blanket and let me know everything was going to be okay. No matter what.

After a couple of weeks, I found myself more at peace with Kenya's departure. I knew that she was surely in a better place. A place with endless Philly cheesesteaks - a place free from pain.

I didn't want to forget Kenya but I found myself being swallowed up by what was in front of me. My day-to-day stuff. School. Alyssa.

Life continues for the living. Even for the dying-living (me). You can't just stop. Everything is always in motion. Like a river. If you're rowing upstream, you gotta keep going. If you stop, then you get pulled back by the current. Forward to backward. Either way, there's motion.

Movement.

Ascend. *Descend.*

TO. FRO.

UP. DOWN.

TOPSY. TURVY.

It never stops.

Race to the end

With Kenya gone, my own mortality was more real to me than ever. I had to prioritise. Like it or not, time was ticking. And I had to cram life in. Kenya's orders. Live my 'best life' in whatever limited time I had left. I knew that I couldn't dillydally and put the Alyssa thing off another second. I had to put it to bed and move on. And in order to do that, I had to confront her.

So we set up the RJ (restorative justice) meeting. I won't take you through the excruciating details of everything that took place, but you already know that I took Option 1.

I sat in a room with Mr K and the indisputable star slash villain of this story, Alyssa Butt Breath Anderson. It felt like some kind of stand-off. Like the final scene in one of those old John Wayne cowboy movies.

This is it. This, my friends, is what they call the 'resolution' of the story that is my life. I was on the edge of my seat. I bet you are too. How would it all turn out?

Mr K had coached me on the language I should use. I wanted to ask her why she had targeted me. Why she had decided to subject me to unrelenting, ongoing, horrible abuse. But I couldn't use those words. I had to use non-threatening, non-blaming, direct words which meant the same thing but didn't make her feel defensive. I've always known about the power of words. But this whole orchestrated face-off, where I had to choose my words ever so carefully, made me think about it on a

d

e

e

p

e

r

level.

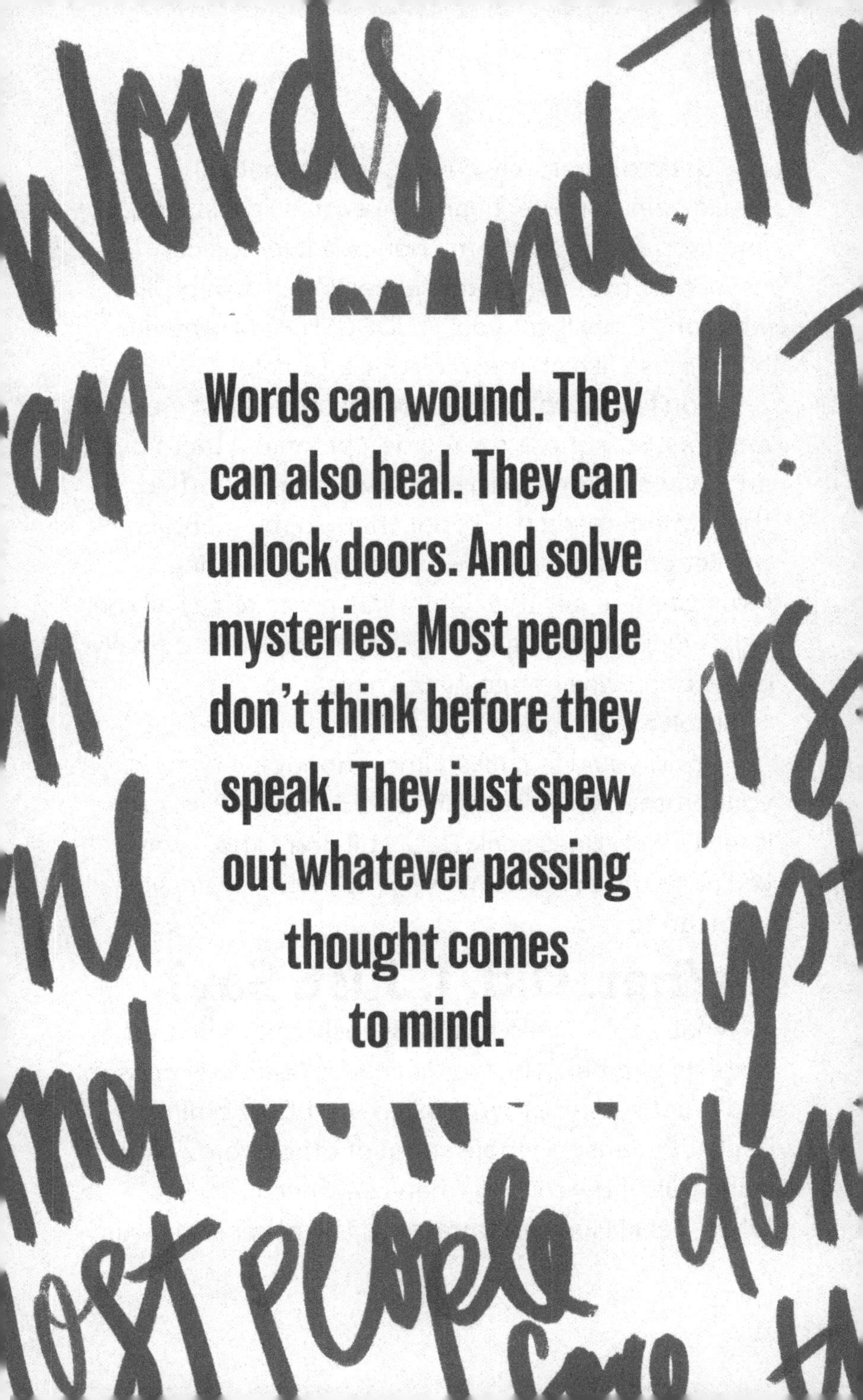

Words can wound. They can also heal. They can unlock doors. And solve mysteries. Most people don't think before they speak. They just spew out whatever passing thought comes to mind.

Others deliberately choose words that will cause pain. You ever heard the expression 'sticks and stones may break my bones but words can never hurt me'? What nonsense! Words can be like weapons. They'll get you, *WHOOOSH*, right where it hurts most, like an arrow hitting a target.

I didn't want to hurt Alyssa anymore. I just wanted answers. So, I chose my words. I practised them over and over again in my mind. Ordered and shuffled them, memorised them, put them in my mental pocket and took them with me to the meeting. I was going to get this right. I was going to say all the right words in the right order. My moment had finally come and I was not going to mess it up.

I took a deep breath . . .

'I know your life sucks. I know about everything, your brother, your mum, the accident. And I'm sorry. It really, truly does suck. But I still don't know why you're so mean to me. Why? Why? Whyyyy are you so mean to me?'

What. Did. I. Just. Say?

What a total brain fart. Obviously that didn't go quite as planned. The words I had so carefully chosen and practised must have fallen out of my brain pocket because a whole string of other words came flying out of my mouth when I saw her. All those 'whys'. Eeek! How embarrassing. The other issue was that I also lost control of my tear ducts. As I was scrambling for my misplaced words, I started crying. Also not part of the plan. My heart raced. My brain hurt. It wouldn't even go on a break like it usually does in times of crisis.

Mr K looked startled. His eyes all round like doughnuts. This was not what he was expecting. Alyssa's face went blank. She stared at me. Not even a mean stare. Or a 'how dare you' stare. Or an 'I'm gonna skin you alive and eat your flesh with a dash of Tabasco sauce after this is over' stare.

A blank stare.

Nothing behind the eyes. I was used to mean Alyssa. I was even used to fake 'nice' Alyssa. But this was new territory. She was kind of like a zombie. A robot. Why was she like this?

Mr K tried to encourage a response from her.

'Alyssa, would you like to respond to Ana?'

But he was unsuccessful too. She had checked out. There was something eerie about the deadness in her eyes. Mr K and I exchanged baffled looks. After what seemed like an eternity of awkward, painful silence, she finally spoke.

Slap in the face

It wasn't an actual slap in the face but her words hurt like one. She was calm as she spoke. No, she wasn't sorry. And she didn't care how her actions had affected me. She didn't care that I was dying and she had no plans to 'make things right' between us. But she understood that things had escalated and that she could get into serious trouble, so the bullying had to end. She agreed to that part, at least. Almost like a cold-hearted killer on death row, who has no option other than to stop.

In a desperate attempt to appeal to her humanity, I told her that I had seen her care for her brother. That Al and I had spied on her. That I knew she was capable of love because I had seen it with my own eyes. But that was met with another blank stare. Again in a calm and scarily composed manner she told me that she didn't want my 'understanding'. She didn't want my 'forgiveness'. She said that tormenting me had been fun for her for a long time but that recently I'd actually become a burden. That she'd be relieved to 'let me loose'. Mr K kept trying to correct her. Surely, because she was going through

such a difficult time at home, she was lashing out. She was hurting too, he suggested. She didn't mean what she said. Deep down, she was, of course, sorry. Wasn't she?

Nope.

Alyssa refused any kind of apology. There was no remorse. No happily ever after, fairytale ending for us, I'm afraid. Just another slap in the face after all the many other slaps in the face.

But one good thing came from it. After that day, Alyssa didn't bother me anymore. No more selfies, no more nasty words. No spitting. No attention at all. Not even a sideways glance as we passed each other in the corridors. She didn't have to wait for me to die because I was dead to her already. It was like she just erased me from her orbit. It wasn't even a deliberate avoidance; it was as though she didn't even register me. I had been deleted from the hard drive of her brain. I had vanished. Just like that.

JUST
LIKE
THAT?

No, no, **nooooo!** This cannot be how the Butt Breath story ends. She can't just waltz into my life, ruin it, and then leave without even a half-hearted apology. This would not do. I rejected this turn of events. This stupid, meaningless conclusion. I needed an explanation for all those years of torment. And more importantly, I wanted to know why I had become invisible to her now. Why she had turned into a zombie.

Poor Al listened to me churn through this for hours and hours. He listened and didn't talk. Which is extremely rare for him. When I was all exhausted and talked out, he sat me down and with a serious, intense look, he said:

'Have you ever had one of those dreams when you're at school and everything is normal and you suddenly realise that you're butt naked?'

'Not now, Al.' I wasn't in the mood for his usual distractions.

'Stay with me. I'm going somewhere with this.'

I sank back into the couch. 'Okay, go on.'

'You're just cruising along, going from Maths to English, and then your heart drops because you realise that you're wearing a T-shirt and NOTHING ELSE. Your bits are flipping and flopping . . .'

'AL!'

'... and you're pulling your T-shirt down in a panic and everyone around you is acting all normal, as if nothing unusual is happening.'

By then Al was re-enacting the dream, pulling his shirt down, talking dramatically. It wasn't meant to be funny but I was in stitches.

'The breeze is blowing on your bare butt cheeks and you're running as fast as you can to get away from the school and everyone in it.'

'Where are you going with this deeply disturbing dream recollection?'

'Can't you see? This is exactly how Alyssa's feeling!'

'Naked?!'

'She's exposed! You know her secret. Her other life. The sad and painful life she's somehow managed to hide from the whole world. So, yes, she feels naked. And that's freaking her out. That's why she's ignoring you. Erasing you. Because that's easier than falling apart and admitting that she's scared and broken. Being mean is her weapon against this cruel and unfair world.'

Al was right. I had been Alyssa's punching bag. And now that I knew her secret, she had to hide from me. Al continued.

'Hurt people, hurt people. That's not an echo. People who've been hurt, sometimes hurt others in the hope that maybe that'll numb their own pain. But it never does. Alyssa Anderson is a sad and mean person. And she'll never give you the answers you want, she'll never be sorry. You really shouldn't waste your time trying to change her. Or wishing she was different. Pack your bags and move on, Ana. Life's too short. You know that better than anybody.'

At that moment, Al was my Gandalf. My Dumbledore. My very own Yoda. I felt the force of his words. Wise and true. They soothed my soul and allowed me to breathe . . .

He was right. Alyssa's cruelty towards me was, in fact, not about me at all. It was about her. It was her burden to carry. And it was heavy. Realising this suddenly made me feel detached. Liberated. I was finally able to unhook the chains that had tied us together all these years. I released the tormented bird from its cage. And I was free, at last.

I stood up and hugged Al. I hugged him as hard and as tight as I could. So tight that he started to laugh.

'Yeah, yeah . . . I know. I love me too. Now let's go get a burger. I'm starving.' I laughed too. Of course he was starving. Al was *always* starving.

Full circle

And there you have it, people. The saga that had plagued me for so much of my life was over. And it didn't end as I had hoped. There was no satisfying resolution like you see in movies. No one had the 'last word'. There was no 'slow clap' moment. Nobody ran through the streets of New York, in the rain, to deliver a big emotional speech about why things were the way they were. (Unless you count Al's naked speech – which I know he'd love!)

No, this was not how real life worked.

I had to accept that not all stories have a neat, satisfying ending. You can't wrap up everything in life and put a pretty bow on it.

Some things remain unresolved.

Some pain never heals.

Everyone is on their own journey.

The point is to focus on our own path and not on other people's. To make our journey as intricate and beautiful and interesting as possible. To stock up on all the gifts as we exit through the gift shop of life. Speaking of gifts . . .

Gifts galore

Last week I went snorkelling with Al. It was one of the things on my bucket list and my mum arranged it with his mum, paid for the whole thing and surprised me one morning by putting a snorkel next to my bowl of porridge.

It was a warm day but the water was FREEZING, which strangely made it more fun. By this stage, I had a bunch of tubes permanently attached to my body but the doctors allowed them to be detached long enough for us to go for a dip. A proper dip. An absolutely freezing, life-affirming, thrilling look under the sea.

I saw such beauty hidden under the water. A glorious marine life that exists literally under the surface of the sea. A parallel world, right under our noses. Maybe when I die, I won't go far . . . maybe I'll just take a sideways step into another life that is right within reach? I was amazed at what I saw. Butterfly fish, cod, angelfish and clown fish, to name a few.

Al had an underwater camera and was madly snapping away. We actually attempted selfies with fishies. It was brilliant. I've never laughed so hard.

Side note: laughing under water is tricky business!

The gifts kept rolling in . . .

Freaky Fridays – scary movie nights at Dad and Wanda's. I got to pick the scariest films and make my chosen people watch them with me. My sibs were too small for horror flicks so they were excused, but Al, Mum, Dad, Wanda, Plastic Pat, Ekua and me would load up the popcorn bowls and I'd subject them to all kinds of horror – starting with *A Nightmare on Elm Street*. Freddy Krueger is both terrifying and hilarious.

I'd be laughing

so hard as I watched Al almost pee his pants from fear.

Then there were my 'writing days'. The greatest gift. You already know that this is my English assignment, now long overdue, but what you should also know is that by writing this, I'm fulfilling one of my greatest life goals. For as long as I can remember, I have wanted to be a writer. I used to write short stories, comics, essays or just diary entries. Words bring me peace. So, this book is definitely a bucket list tick. My 'writing days' have been some of the happiest days of my life. Mum works so hard to make sure I have all that I need for them. She gave me the most beautiful mahogany desk which I've put in my room, right next to the window. I'm sitting at it right now. She brings me Persian tea, of course. Also chocolate, dumplings, liquorice and whatever else takes my fancy. Unlike most people in their final days or months, I don't seem to have lost my appetite. In fact, I've been slowly gaining weight since coming back from America – which makes my parents super happy. Mum is always there with food and love in abundance.

So, I get to eat. And write. Two of my favourite things. Al is often by my side, partaking of the eating and giving me notes on my book. Always asking where and how he appears and if I could give him more 'lines', more storylines, and his very own chapters, even.

'Make me sound funny. Am I funny? I better be funny.'

'You're very funny, Al,' I promise him.

'And tough. I can't *just* be a funny guy. I wanna be strong. And ripped. Like Dwayne Johnson. Can you make me like The Rock?'

Honestly, if he had his way, this whole book would be about him with me as an incidental character who makes a cameo appearance from time to time. Unfortunately for Al, though, this story *is* about me. And the last year of my life. I don't know if it will ever get published but if you're reading it, then chances are that it did! And I'm rejoicing just at the very thought of that!

Parting words

I don't want you to remember me as Ana, the dying girl. I want to be remembered as Ana, the girl who was blessed with life.

The one thing everyone says to you when you're dying is 'I'm so sorry'.

Over and over and over again.

AND OVER AND OVER AND OVER AND OVER

OVER AND OVER AND OVER AND OVER AND

OVER AND OVER AND OVER AND OVER AND

OVER AND OVER AND OVER OVER AND OVER

AND OVER AND OVER AND OVER AND OVER

AND OVER AND OVER AND OVER AND OVER

AND OVER AND OVER AND OVER AND OVER

AND OVER AND OVER AND OVER AND OVER

AND OVER AND OVER AND OVER AND OVER

People assume that because I'm dying, my life must totally suck. But my power lies in my happiness. And I'm choosing to be happy. Every single day that I get to walk this earth is a bonus, so why be miserable? It just doesn't make any sense. So, bring on the joy, I say!

And look, I'm just as confused as anyone by how we're supposed to make our life matter. How to make 'living' a form of art. A dance. A poem. A ninja movie. But I reckon beauty comes from just trying.

I've had my share of ups and downs in life. From dealing with Butt Breath Anderson to rockin' out in the school corridors to surviving my parents' icky divorce to meeting Al in the canteen line on my first day at school.

I'm grateful for all of it. All of it was meant to be. I don't think there are any 'accidents' in life. Whatever happens was somehow crafted and sent to you by design. So, as I approach the next chapter of my existence, here are my parting words:

In the end, none of it matters.

And all of it matters.

LIFE IS DEATH AND DEATH IS LIFE.

IT IS ALL PART OF THE SAME CONTINUUM.

THERE IS NO REAL SEPARATION.

DESPITE POPULAR BELIEF, WE DON'T LIVE SEPARATE LIVES.

WE ARE ALL INTERCONNECTED.

YOU ARE ME.

AND I AM YOU.

AND WE ARE ALL PART OF SOMETHING BIGGER.

SO, DON'T SWEAT THE SMALL STUFF, PEOPLE. OR THE BIG STUFF, FOR THAT MATTER. DON'T 'STRUT AND FRET YOUR HOUR UPON THE STAGE' AS SHAKESPEARE WOULD SAY.

LIVE EACH DAY LIKE IT'S YOUR LAST.

AND DON'T FORGET TO CHECK OUT ALL THE GIFTS BEFORE IT'S YOUR TIME TO EXIT — STAGE LEFT.